I0610068

Murmurs in the Dark

MURMURS
IN THE
DARK
THIRTEEN GHOSTLY TALES
FROM BOOK VIEW CAFÉ

EDITED BY
MARISSA DOYLE & SHANNON PAGE

Book View Café

MURMURS IN THE DARK: THIRTEEN GHOSTLY
TALES FROM BOOK VIEW CAFÉ
Copyright © 2021 by Book View Café

Edited by Marissa Doyle and Shannon Page
All rights reserved.

No part of this book may be reproduced in any form or by
any electronic or mechanical means, including information
storage and retrieval systems, without written permission
from the authors, except for the use of brief quotations in a
book review.

This is a work of fiction. Any references to historical events,
real people, or real locales are used fictitiously. Other names,
characters, places, and incidents are productions of the
authors' imagination, and any resemblance to actual events
or locales or persons, living or dead, is entirely coincidental.

Published by Book View Café
304 S. Jones Blvd., Suite 2906
Las Vegas, NV 89107

ISBN: 978-1-61138-991-3

Cover art by Ravenborn
Cover Design by Marissa Doyle

Foreword Copyright © 2021 Marissa Doyle and Shannon
Page.

"The Summer House: a Fable" by Chaz Brenchley.
Copyright © 2021 Chaz Brenchley

"With Stars in Her Eyes" by Alma Alexander. Copyright © 2021 Alma Alexander.

"Love in the Company of Ghosts" by Steven Popkes. Copyright ©2021 Steven Popkes

"House Is Where the Heart Is" by Marissa Doyle. Copyright © 2021 Marissa Doyle.

"La Dame Blanche" by Brenda W. Clough. Copyright © 2021 Brenda W. Clough.

"Given to the Sunrise" by Dave Smeds. Copyright © 2021 Dave Smeds.

"Lideric" by Jennifer Stevenson. Original publication: *Only a Paper Moon*, Book View Café, 2020. Copyright © 2020 Jennifer Stevenson.

"Violence Begets..." by Paul Piper. Copyright © 2021 Paul Piper.

"The Nature of Things by Maya Kaathryn Bohnhoff. Original publication: *Baen's Universe*, Vol. 1, #1, December 2006. Copyright © 2006 Maya Kaathryn Bohnhoff.

"Golden Spider Beetles" by Shannon Page. Copyright © 2021 Shannon Page.

"Borrowed Places" by K.E. Kimbriel. Copyright © 2021 K.E. Kimbriel.

"The Waking of Angantyr" by Marie Brennan. Original publication: *Heroic Fantasy Quarterly*, #2, October 2009.Copyright © 2009 Marie Brennan.

"It All Ends with a Game of Croquet" by Jill Zeller. Copyright © 2021 Jill Zeller.

Table of Contents

Foreword

Book View Café has put out many anthologies of our members' short pieces over the years, collections built around fantasy, steampunk, science fiction, romance, and other themes and genres…but somehow—goodness knows why—we've never gotten around to doing anything with horror.

This collection remedies that oversight. Because who doesn't love a good ghost story?

Murmurs in the Dark presents thirteen ghostly tales, the majority of which have never before been published. Like ghosts themselves, these stories take many forms. Some (such as Paul Piper's "Violence Begets…" and Shannon Page's "Golden Spider Beetles") give the reader a properly other-worldly chill. Others are lyrical (Chaz Brenchley's "The Summer House: a Fable"), epic (Marie Brennan's "The Waking of Angantyr"), historical (Dave Smed's "Given to the Sunrise" and Brenda W. Clough's "La Dame Blanche"), and even humorous (Maya Kaathryn Bohnhoff's "The Nature of Things" and Marissa Doyle's "House Is Where the Heart Is".) As varied and wonderful, in fact, as our authors.

When we first announced that we wanted to put together a ghost story anthology, we didn't know what we would get from our membership, apart from being certain that we were in for some excellent reading. And we weren't disappointed. Now that the anthology is complete, we are absolutely thrilled (and just a little shivery).

We hope you'll enjoy it as well!

Marissa Doyle
Shannon Page
July 2021

The Summer House: a Fable

Chaz Brenchley

Oh, he was golden, in my house that summer: or better than golden, he was radiant, bright and burning in the perfect moment of his youth and knowing it, knowing that it would never be better than this.

Not that he cared, or needed to. Why would he ever move on from this? He was like an ant in honey, caught in the sweetest instance of his life.

Me, I was twenty years older, twenty years darker and more bitter. We were, I suppose, an exercise in contrasts. You could say that we were complementary, that we could each complete the other.

I did say so, when I was driven to it, when I was goaded.

Juliet was my oldest friend, and she did love to goad me. All my adulthood she'd watched me with a species of amused astonishment, and delighted in poking me just where I was tender.

"It can't last," she said, laughing at me. "It is magnificent, you're extraordinary together; but it can't last.

It's a folly, a *folie à deux*, he's as culpable as you are. I give it the summer, no more. Three glorious months, and goodbye. You're meteoric, you and Jack; and you know the thing about meteors? They don't rise, my love. It's not about rise and fall. Meteors crash to earth, that's what they do. One beautiful blaze, it's a privilege to watch, but it never will be anything other than catastrophic. And you really, really don't want to be underneath. Trying to catch them as they fall, give them a kinder landing? Seriously not a good idea."

That was Juliet: practical, clear-sighted, confident in her own analysis. Promising not to be there at the end.

I wasn't about to argue. I agreed with her, in more or less every particular: only not in her unspoken conclusion, that all this was a bad thing. His eternal summer should not fade, should not be allowed to. A boy has to keep his tan topped up. Come the autumn, I knew he'd be off to some other hemisphere that tipped the other way, dragging his daisy-chain of broken hearts behind him, mine only the latest, not the last.

Except that I was forewarned and not liable to break, in the heart or otherwise. I don't chase sunshine, I don't pine for my lost youth. Come a change of season, I have my winter house to dwell in, in the valley, on my own.

This, though: this was high summer, high on the hill. We had views with breakfast, owl-calls with our Armagnac. Betweentimes we might run into town for a meal or a movie or a party, an art gallery with his friends or with mine, but I thought it was best when people came up to the house, long idle days of scratch lunches and gourmet dinners, cocktails on the terrace, those conversations that you get between youth and experience, all heat and laughter and unbridgeable gulfs.

One afternoon, he said, "Gideon? Can I have a

swimming pool on my terrace too, when I grow up?"

"You? You never will grow up," I said. "Eternally nineteen."

"I'm twenty-three."

"That's what I mean. You're stuck already."

"Yeah, yeah. Ant in honey. I know, you told me."
And he sprawled at my feet, half naked and all glorious,
all child, ready to be told again.

I said, "Not that. What I mean, to qualify as an
adult, you need to stop moving. Cherish stillness, put
down roots. It's not in your nature. You'll always be
looking for the next thing, eyes on the distant horizon,
waiting for the lightning to strike. When are you going
to have the time to acquire a swimming pool? Where
are you going to put it? Oh, you'll never be short of a
pool to swim in, Jack, it just won't ever be your own."

----◆----

The corollary of that, of course, was that I wouldn't
always be picking up his sodden and abandoned towels
from the poolside. Someone would, beyond question;
just not me. While it lasted, though, at least I could
enjoy it. Beauty may only be skin-deep, but heedless-
ness goes all the way through. It was a legitimate
privilege to pick up after him, to gather his neglected
things, to be careful of what he gave no thought to. It
allowed me access to something that ran core-deep in
him, one aspect of his soul.

And no, I did not say any of that to Juliet.

Picking up towels in late afternoon sun, wringing
water in a spatter from his trunks, I caught something
in the corner of my eye, a cold shadow rising in the
water.

And looked round, startled, sure until that moment
that the pool had been empty, that Jack and all his

cohort had gone indoors in search of drinks and cricket scores and snacks.

And was right, of course, there was no one, nothing in the water: only in my eye, in my memory, a vagrant hint of purpose. Some trick of breeze and light, no doubt; but sunlight dazzles on a wind-ruffed pool, and this had been a darkness, an absence, like lost information, data gone astray.

I shivered, momentarily as chilly in my body as the thought of it was chilly in my head, unreachable by sunlight.

———◆———

It must still have been working on me an hour later. Jack touched my arm, and I startled almost out of my skin. Just for a moment it had felt like someone else's touch altogether, as though a whole cold army had reached to touch me through his fingers.

"Steady, soldier," he said, laughing at me, holding a cocktail back ostentatiously out of my reach. "What's got into you?"

"I don't know. Nothing," but my hand was rubbing at my arm where he'd touched me, and I didn't want to look, in case I saw black bruises rising to mark where each separate finger had lain. That was how it felt, like the love-bites of my adolescence, suction-bruises where something had been drawn out of me. "Is that drink mine?"

"It is—but only if you pay attention to our collective wit and wisdom. You've been missing in action ever since we came in from the pool." He was scolding, light and easy, but I wasn't convinced. Golden boys aren't good at misdirection. I thought there was something wary in him suddenly, a watchfulness that didn't suit.

I smiled and shrugged and played the world-weary

sophisticate. "The only thing I'm missing is the sight of pretty young things splashing about in sunshine."

"Pervert."

We grinned at each other in mutual dishonesty, me pretending not to be disturbed and him pretending to believe me; the drink met my reaching hand, but I didn't really want it. The whole point of cocktails at sunset is the kick of strong spirits and the shock of ice, that double strike against a warm sobriety, and I'd been twice struck already, once by bewilderment and once by the cold dread that came with it.

Drink and company and the pleasures they entail: these touches of panic, moments of doomsaying are easily drowned or buried, so long as there is alcohol to blur the senses and talk to batter at the mind. It's in the silent reaches of the night that they recur, and that night we talked late and long, or I did, just to fend them off. I talked about what was fixed and solid, places I'd been and things I'd done, people I'd loved and left or loved and lost, anything that was over. Houses too, I know I talked about houses. Particularly my winter house, down in the valley. Perhaps I even asked him if he'd like to see it one day, tomorrow, we could walk down tomorrow, just the two of us...

If I did do that, he certainly said no. I must have known, he wouldn't want to see it. We both knew he wouldn't be here, come winter. Why would he let himself be shown pleasures he would never taste, comforts he would never know? Jack was all about immediacy, life undeferred, whatever lay under his hand.

I lay under his hand, and took pleasure in it, as I had to do; he was here, now, and it wouldn't last. That was understood.

Summer is about separation, peeling, exposure. That
was also understood. One by one, our friends fell away
from us, like petals falling from a flower. All his friends
were new friends, he never kept hold of anyone from
one summer to the next; easy come easy go, they went
surfing in Cornwall or hitching to Greece, beach-
bumming in Thailand or volunteering for some planet-
saving eco project in Africa. All my friends were old
friends, hoarded for decades; they migrated to their
second homes in France, or else flew off to a conference
in Japan, a posting in New Zealand, some new flare-up
in an old exhausted war.

Juliet never goes anywhere, but even she went that
year. She didn't want to be anywhere near the valley,
she said, when I came crashing down to earth. We
found ourselves pretty much alone, then, Jack and I, in
the dog-end of the heat. Which was perfect, or should
have been: good company to start the summer with and
then solitude, intensity, focus. It's the structure of great
jazz, which is the structure of great summers. I even
caught myself singing to myself, in and around the
house when he was sleeping.

Singing one day as I went to shave, I tilted the
mirror to catch the light—and almost screamed. I know
I made some kind of noise, just as I know I jumped
back, physically shocked; and my fingers trembled on
the chrome as I reached to touch it again, to tilt it again,
as I forced my eyes to look again.

The first time, where I should have been looking at
my own reflection, I had seen nothing: an expression of
nothingness, rather, a grey and sucking blankness in the
mortal form of man.

This time, the second time, I saw a face I didn't
recognise, and that was worse. Old and grey and pale,

he stared at me like the bitter residue of a life ill-lived, a life that drained and not inspired, that fed nothing but only fed off him. I looked at him and thought of carrion comfort, of despair. What was worse, he looked at me, and I couldn't tell what he was thinking. What was worst, I could see in him altogether too much of myself, lineaments of my face and manner, I thought he was unrecognisably me.

The shaving-mirror has two faces. I turned it, in despair myself, in search of carrion comfort: and found it, because the side that magnified showed me nothing but my own cheek, stubbled and slick with a greasy sweat.

When I had washed—slowly, tremblingly, splashing too much water on the floor—and reached for the razor, looking again, I was shocked again before I could touch blade to face; and that of course was when he walked in to find me.

He smiled, and his fingers stroked my cheek, and again my warm wet skin felt it like the touch of something chill and desiccating; and he said, "What, so sharp you're scared you'll cut yourself, is that the hesitation?"

"No," I said. "Look," and I showed him, right there in the black shadow of a night's growth: first gleam of silver, grey hairs in sudden patches like smeared fingerprints across my cheek.

And he laughed at me, and kissed me—and I swear he felt the shudder that I couldn't suppress, and it was an effort even to try to pass it off as vanity exposed.

Later—was it the same day or was it another day, another week? I forget, time blurs like fingerprints, all the grip it has upon us once it's gone—we were talking and he was teasing me, trying to measure my experience, so many other lovers and had I ever counted? Which was another way to say *grey hairs*, and his fingers strayed across my scalp as if in search, until I stopped abruptly and said, "You never talk about your past."

"Oh," he said, "I'm still a baby, next to you. Not enough water under the bridge, I don't have any stories worth the telling."

There are lies and lies. Some are social niceties, and some are wish fulfilment. This was just evasion, and I called him on it.

"Don't give me that. Tell me something true."

He sulked for a moment, but I outwaited him. Young men can't deal with silence; sometimes that's the only weapon that we have.

He said, "I don't like to talk about it," which was silence under another name, a demand I was in no mood to gratify.

I said, "That's not fair. I talk a lot about where I've been, who I've been with, and you never do. Oh, you're entitled to your privacy, of course, you can have your secrets—but you can't just pull a curtain behind you and say that everything back there is no-go. Where do you come from, Jack? What histories have you brought into my house?"

"Best not to ask," he said. "Truly."

"Come on. Everybody has sorrows, disappointments..."

"...tragedies, regrets," he finished for me. "Of course. But why look back, why dwell on them? Why share? I like to look forward."

"The man who doesn't remember his history..."

"...is condemned to repeat it." He was in the mood to interrupt, clearly: sharp and edgy, like a knife. "Right. I know. So's everyone else. What goes around, comes around; it's just a rule, it's not a revelation." And then, turning his head to gaze out across the pool, across the valley, all that dulling distance, he said, "Seriously, Gideon? There are some stones it's better not to lift. Let me be elusive and mysterious, let the dead past bury its dead."

I could do that; it's one of the charms of youth, after all, that they can be so gauche with secrets and so determined to be interesting.

My summer house, though, it's all about clarity and focus. You can see a long way from the top of the hill, and summer light is brutally revealing. He didn't come out so often now, to sit with me in the sun; and when he did he covered up, he wore a robe over his trunks or dressed in shirt and slacks. More often he stayed indoors or else in the pool, where broken water could break up the light, where I could only see him distorted. Either way, I said his tan would fade, but he just shrugged as though it didn't matter. And went indoors with his cellphone and his secrets, and I thought maybe he was already packing inside his head, travelling light, shedding unnecessary load. Chasing cheap tickets on the internet, picking up contacts in Melbourne or Tonga or Tierra del Fuego. Not that he'd go yet, he'd need to wait on the unruly sun, but I thought he was making ready.

Me, I stayed where I sat, and watched a cloud's shadow drift down the valley towards me.

And looked up, into the clearest of summer skies, not a cloud to be seen; and still saw that shadow coming on, blind and remorseless, marching upslope towards me, terrible as an army with banners.

It slid over my neighbour's fields, over my own hedge, my garden; it engulfed the terrace, the swimming pool, myself.

Not a cloud-shadow at all, nothing so amorphous or meaningless or benign. What the cloud doeth, the Lord knoweth; the cloud knoweth not. This—well, this knew. It had intensity, purpose, focus. It came on like a shadow, but not like any shadow of this world. Something else, that stood between another light and me: someones else, rather, other people. I could almost hear their whispers, almost feel them jostle me as they passed, over and around and through. I shuddered, bone-deep, as though they marched in my marrow. And felt them go on into the house, and for a moment I was afraid for Jack.

Then I was afraid for myself.

Then I got to my feet in a cold grey light, as though the sun lay shrouded. I could see it yet, and the sky was just as clear, only obscured somehow, veiled by a mist that wasn't quite there. The air had been warm and heavy; now it was whip-sharp, thin and piercing.

I found Jack waiting for me in neutral space, the spare bedroom, the room we never used. He had his rucksack out on the bed there, half full already. Neither of us mentioned that. I was shivering where he was sweaty, as though we shared a fever, but in honesty I thought that we shared nothing now, except this confrontation. Not even memories: he would deny those, if he couldn't actually expunge them. Walk away, don't look back. Never take your old friends with you.

I said, "I'll ask you one more time. What have you brought into my house?"

He sulked at me, eternally nineteen. "Nothing."

"That's not true."

"I don't bring them. They follow me…"

And he fled them, presumably, down the nights and down the days. From one hemisphere to another he outflew them, and they chased. He clung to summer, to the sunlight, to the heat; and they caught him regardless, and closed this bitter chill around him like a curse. Even the sun's hard hammer couldn't break it, all he could do was run. Again. And again, and...

There was an obvious next question, *who are they?*—but even if I could have depended on his answer, I still thought I didn't need to ask. I'd always understood that chain of broken hearts he trailed in his wake, but this was more. I remembered the shadow in the swimming pool, the face in the shaving-mirror. I thought of myself grown absent in my own body, lost and grey; I thought of how his touch had felt so chill, so draining. How my cheek sported an ash-white brand that I shaved off every morning.

How ash was what remained after fire, dull desiccated residue, once the life was gone.

How he was so intensely physical, golden and perfect beside me, already younger than his years: as a boy might be who battened onto older men—leech-like, vampiric—and took something essential from them. Nothing so simple as blood, nothing so homely or so easily replaced. Something that would leave his victims—them, us—losing definition, losing clarity, losing colour. And hungry for it, and coming after, like creditors in pursuit of a bankrupt, trying helplessly to reclaim what he had already spent.

If these were ghosts that milled about us now, I thought they were the ghosts of people not yet dead, which was worse somehow: some hollow cast-off, some echo personality sent in pursuit or simply doomed to be dragged after, not cut free. Perhaps he hauled it with him, what he fled; perhaps they weren't sendings at all, perhaps he ran from a clatter of his own making, like a cat with empty tins tied to its tail.

He would take nothing more from me, nothing that mattered. His fingers spilled clothes and toiletries as he packed, the first graceless actions I'd seen in him; he looked something less than beautiful, or perhaps something more, a haggard kind of beauty, as though his ivory bones were showing beneath that eternal tan.

If we talked at all, I don't remember it. What was there to say?

He left, is all that matters. He left, and I watched him go; and then—alone, necessarily, because all my friends had fled the clamour of this collapse—I did some packing of my own. I packed up my summer house, even there in the height of summer. I didn't notice exactly when the chill left, when my uninvited guests understood that Jack had moved on and so must they; I only noticed at last that it was warm again, that I'd been sweating for a while as I worked, that I was alone another way.

I packed and left my summer house too soon, drained the swimming pool and moved down to the valley. I settled into my winter home, into the shadows and the noise of river, noise of traffic, noise of other people's lives around me. I found some shelter in that, perhaps, while I huddled in dark rooms and waited for my friends to find me. And already, already there was something in my spirit questing after him: as the addict turns to the needle, as the needle turns to the north.

———————◆———————

Chaz Brenchley has been making a living as a writer since the age of eighteen. He is the author of nine thrillers, two fantasy series, two novels about a haunting house and two collections, most recently the Lambda Award-winning *Bitter Waters*. He has also published fantasy as Daniel Fox, and urban fantasy as Ben Macallan. He lost count of his short stories long ago; a "best of" collection will be published in 2021. He is also currently publishing a series of girls' boarding-school stories set on Mars. His work has won multiple awards; it has been translated into languages from Chinese to Estonian. In his fifties he married and moved from Newcastle to California, with two squabbling cats and a famous teddy bear.

He can be found on Facebook, Twitter and Patreon.

About the story

So 'way back in 2004, m'friend the poet Sean O'Brien and I were in our favourite pub in Newcastle (the Bodega, since you ask), drinking pints and setting the world to rights, as you do; and Sean said, "What you and I should do, Chaz, we should write ghost stories and give a reading at Christmas."

Even at the time, I was fairly sure that he meant on the M R James model, where he'd invite a dozen of his friends to his rooms at Cambridge and read them around the firelight; but Sean said it to me, in the centre of Newcastle, and I had An Idea.

So when we left the pub I went to my favourite place on the planet, the Lit and Phil, which is properly the Literary and Philosophical Society of Newcastle upon Tyne, but is actually a private library, a Georgian building with a Victorian interior (we don't talk about the dreadful Fire of 1850); and I buttonholed the Librarian, and said basically, "Me, Sean, one more for balance, probably our friend Gail-Nina; ghost stories; Christmas." And she said, "Oh, yes. Yes please," she said.

So then there I was, walking up the hill towards m'house, feeling very bouncily full of myself because I'd just arranged a gig and it was going to be fun; and I met two friends of mine coming down the hill, and one of them was a (very) small publisher of very beautiful books, and the other made her living by drawing together artists and venues and sources of funding. And I bounced happily all over them, crying "Gig!", and he said, "Ghost stories, hmm? I'd be interested in publishing those," and she said, "What you need is Arts Council funding..."

So I turned around and we all three went back to the pub, and had a business meeting; and we ended up with a fully-funded free event, with three writers and musicians in the gallery and a slim but beautiful volume with a CD tucked into the back. It booked out so quickly before Christmas that we had to repeat it after Christmas, played to a full house again and could probably have repeated it at least one time more.

So of course we did it again, and then again the year after, with encores each time. After that there was no more funding, but we carried on the events anyway, because we enjoyed them so much; and eventually we figured out that there was totally an audience for another event at midsummer, so we added that into the roster.

And obviously I wanted to write a summer story for our first summer event, and I've always been fascinated by the notion of having one house for the summer and another for the winter, so I went ahead and did that, and "The Summer House" is the result.

With Stars in Her Eyes

Alma Alexander

I'd known her all my life.

Oh, I'd never seen her. I *glimpsed* her. When I was very young, I'd glance past the tall hollyhocks which grew along the garden fence of the widow who lived next door to us, quite on her own, and there she was, the girl who should have never been there, her hair floating even though there was no wind, catching my eye with an enigmatic little grin. Or I'd be in a train, the small me being packed off back to my boarding school after the summer hols, with my parents just having been booted off by the conductor, and I'd be sitting there with my feet dangling above the floor and looking out of the window, and there she would be, standing behind them, waving me away. Or there would be a whisper in the wind which sounded like my name and I'd turn, circling, convinced I'd heard someone call me, and there was that hair, disappearing slowly behind a tree or around a corner, leaving behind a fading and knowing smile, like a cartoon Cheshire Cat. I couldn't possibly tell you what colour the hair was—maybe it was different every time. And her eyes changed colour too. They did that with the season. Her eyes would be a tender green in spring, a mellow molten golden amber wheat shade in the summer, a rich mahogany with touches of maple-leaf red in the fall, a pale ice blue in winter. Or maybe she would turn up with blue eyes in mid-summer, just to throw you. She'd do that kind of thing.

I told someone about her once, like I'm telling you now—when I was twelve, maybe—and it was a grown-up I'd trusted, but not family. Not my parents. Never them. I could never talk about something like this to them—not the people who decided I would be better off at boarding school aged seven. They took care that I had all the necessities of survival, but nothing that I needed to *live*; I always felt vaguely guilty for just *existing,* a squirming little inconvenience they packed off with a sigh of relief and got on with the lives I had somehow interrupted by being born unexpectedly—so much later than my siblings, well after my parents thought they were done with having family. They had no time for me, they had already shown me that, and I thought I understood the message completely. I confided in other people. My mother was always too cool and distant to be bothered by childish 'secrets' like this. But the adult whom I did tell about my dream girl listened while I talked, and then tried to tell me about something called 'lucid dreaming'. My companion girl had no name, before that; but afterwards, I started calling her Lucy.

The first time I have a real memory of her was when I was very young—maybe four or five years old— the first real memory I know I can trust. This was real, damn it all. It was real. I know I was practically a *baby*, but it's vivid in my mind, and I will swear to it. The family was on a picnic, on a piece of greensward by the river, it must have been June or July, full summer anyway; the grown-ups were busy setting out the food and us kids, we were all mucking about on the shore. Me, and my brother Ted, and my sisters Lonie (her real name was Leona but nobody would call her that, much to her disgust) and Lizzy—I was the youngest, by a *lot*, and I wasn't really even wanted by my siblings, because I was so in the way and they were obliged to keep an eye on me rather than get on with the things they wanted to do. There was an ancient boat pulled up on the shore, and Ted managed to maneuver it out into the water, and Lizzy said something about it never floating, and I ended up in the boat, somehow, while all the rest of them were on the shore, and the boat not only floated but started to float *away*. And I thought I ought to shout, or call out, or otherwise bring attention to my plight, but all that would come out was a strangled little whimper as I realized that there was a widening ribbon of water between the boat I was in and the river-shore.

And then there was that whisper, of someone calling my name, and I lifted my eyes and saw her—the girl whose name I didn't yet know, back then—standing there ankle deep in the water, with sunlight scintillating around her narrow ankles like liquid diamond, and she whispered at me, "*Call their names…*"
So I finally did.

"Ted! Lizzy! Lonie…!"

They turned, and saw the boat drifting, and Ted flung himself into the river after it. And we were dragged back into shore, the boat and I, and my sisters, once they were sure I was unharmed and that therefore they would not be brought to account for anything, launched into a withering attack about how I shouldn't be so 'careless' (even though I could never have shifted the boat by myself, so it was in no wise my fault…). I looked around, but she was gone, the girl who had brought me home.

The first time I saw her, I was four. The first time

I named her, I was twelve. Then she followed me through life, lingering at turnstiles, ducking into hiding like a child playing hide-and-seek when I noticed her amongst trees, hopping into taxi cabs and just closing the door as I turned to look almost before I was quite sure it was her...but it always was. There were times that it quite simply seemed to me like she was the burst of sunshine through a bank of cloud, giving me a glimpse of light just when I needed to see it, her hair shining like a star-spangled halo around her face. Sometimes it was just the face, even just the smile, lingering in the edge of a cloud, or scintillating in the tender blue of a springtime sky in the sparkle of sun, disappearing like dust motes into a sunbeam if I tried to look too hard.

She was good at *hiding*...at hiding in plain sight. You could look directly at her, and never see her. You could only ever see her out of the corner of your eye, when you weren't quite expecting her.

Which could only mean that she really was there all the time, probably right in front of me, right where I could not possibly see her if I was looking straight ahead at where I was going.

And I grew addicted to the glimpses...so I stopped looking straight ahead, completely. My life was lived crablike, moving sideways, never quite aiming at a goal directly but sidling up to it from the edges on in, reaching out to grab the thing I was after just as I became certain that absolutely nobody believed that I wanted it...and so I usually got it, because nobody bothered protecting it. I was a walking sneak attack.

Lonie would call me up to ask how I was and I'd come up with something metaphorical, and she'd snort into the phone.

"Nobody can ever get a straight answer out of you," she complained. "I just hope that if you ever really did need something you'd have the sense to call me."

"But I don't need anything," I responded calmly.

Not from her. Not from anyone real.

I was chasing a dream. An angel. An alien. A ghost. A girl called Lucy, always just out of my reach.

My parents lived in something just this side of a mansion, all of their lives. They accumulated— furniture, papers, collections of esoteric things like eggs made out of semiprecious stones which made me think that if I did something weird to them like set them on fire they'd hatch into a bunch of rare and exotic and extinct species like phoenix birds and rocs and the like. My father died when he was relatively young—he barely made it past sixty-five—but my mother lived until a ripe old age, closing in on her century when she finally closed her eyes, still living in the same old house where she'd been rattling around by herself (and a caretaker biddy) for decades after she was widowed. And it then fell to Lonie and me (Lizzy knew way too well how to avoid such things; she'd gone so far as to literally move out of the country so as not to be called upon to participate...and Ted, too, was gone, died young, flung off his motorbike into the path of an oncoming truck many years before...) to deal with the impedimenta of those two lives, accreted in that house like barnacles almost obliterating the shape of an ancient ship's hull. Lonie dealt with the eggs, thankfully, before I could start thinking too hard about what would happen if I stuck them under a broody chicken. We had a man come in and cart away the furniture—the pieces in the rooms, as well as the pieces which sat collecting dust in storage, my parents never apparently having bothered to actually get rid of anything they had replaced. When it came to the paperwork, we made a date to meet at the house, and go through what Mam had left behind.

I suppose you could have called the mausoleum that had been Dad's office organized, after its own fashion. There were *pigeonholes*, I kid you not. And there were filing cabinets with files in them. But the system…was esoteric, if I want to be kind. If there was a system. If it wasn't all just where only the people who needed to access information could do so but any stranger would end up sitting weeping on the floor in a flurry of papers coming down slowly like snow. Lonie and I weren't exactly strangers but the system was a bulwark even against us, the children. There would be two distinct pieces of the same document filed away meticulously and for no apparent reason in two separate places, and the thing only made sense when the two pieces were brought together—and we made magic, and did a lot of that, but I couldn't help wondering how much we were missing, would miss, simply by not being able to find the matching missing half lost somewhere in the labyrinth.

We found Ted's birth certificate, filed with an almost creepy mournful precision together with the death certificate issued after his accident—it was like a portable tombstone, the dates of birth and death carved into the paperwork, *in memoriam*. We found the girls' birth certificates filed together, in a completely different place. And in a third place, there was an unlabeled file that contained what appeared to be the certification of my own arrival into the world.

Except…I'd had to obtain a copy of my birth certificate for official purposes many years before, and I knew what it looked like. This wasn't it. This wasn't the birth certificate I remembered at all.

In fact, there were two documents. One of them was the twin of the one I had in my possession, back in my own (more chaotic but somehow far less confusing) filing system back home. The other...showed... something quite different.

It was a birth certificate for a girl. My date of birth, my exact details, but not me—not the boy. A girl. A girl...who had no name entered in the proper field in the certificate. A ghost girl. Someone whose birth was certified by this document I held in my hand, but someone who had never existed.

My scalp prickled. I knew if I looked up, looked sideways, there she would be, behind the filing cabinet, smiling at me: *Here we are. We meet at last.*

"Lonie..."

"Mmmhm?" She looked up, absorbed in another mound of papers, making two piles in front of her—a discard and a possibly-keep-at-least-for-a-while pile.

I held out the ghost birth certificate. She reached out and took it, and then went very still, staring at it.

"You know something," I said, wishing I sounded less accusing. "What is it, Leona? What's going on there?"

"I didn't know she'd kept a record," Lonie said quietly. "If I'd been the one to lay hands on this...I'd have burned it before you saw it."

"I've seen it now," I said. "Tell me. *Tell* me, Lonie."

"I was only twelve," she said defensively.

"I *know*," I said patiently. "You've always been twelve years older than me. That hasn't changed. But twelve is old enough to know something. Something more than me, clearly. I'd just been born, remember? They couldn't tell me anything, then, and they obviously never thought it was important enough to tell me afterwards."

"They never told me, either," Lonie said, sitting back, letting the birth certificate flutter down into her lap. "I figured it out, much later, when my own babies were born, and Mam was sometimes...odd...about it. I never asked, she never told me directly, but when you were born...well...there were two of you."

"Lonie."

"I mean two babies," Lonie said. "There was you. And then there was something we never spoke about. Something that was here, and was never here. Something that touched us, and went away again."

"Lucy," I said softly.

"What was that?"

There were many things Lonie had not been told. I weighed my own secrets, and held onto them, for now. "Go on," I said.

"Not much more to go on with," Lonie said. "You were supposed to be twins."

"Mam never loved me," I said.

"She did," Lonie said earnestly. "She just didn't...know how not to love the one she never got to hold. It was love you too much, and give you all, or hold onto that loss...and she did...and then she couldn't love you enough. You couldn't help being a reminder, just by existing. I guess she'd look at you and see a shadow beside you, and she couldn't handle it. So she pushed you away."

"I've seen her, too," I said, making the decision.

"Seen...who?"

"I don't know what to call her. The lost soul, I guess. I've kept company with Lucy since I was four years old."

Lonie was looking at me strangely. "Lucy? Who's Lucy? What are you saying?"

So I told her. I told her about the boat on the river—and she remembered that, too. Naturally she had never seen the ghost standing ankle-deep in the sun-sparkling water, calling me back to shore. I told her how I'd seen Lucy hiding in the hollyhocks of the widow's garden. How I'd seen her dart into tree shadows and disappear. How she'd been seeing me off on journeys, or greeting me as I came home from them. How I had carried her, all my life. Or perhaps how she had carried me.

I thought now, if ever, she would be here— watching this, finally coming home. The girl whom they had never really named, apparently—whom they had abandoned in the shadowlands, adrift, nameless, alone. Until she found the only soul that could see her, that would acknowledge her, that would seek her and treasure her and know her, that would let her exist in this world. But she wasn't there. I knew she wasn't there. I'd always known when she was near, and now she was not. I was on my own. It felt at once liberating and terrifying, as though I had been crossing a stream of rushing water by balancing on stepping stones, and one of them had just lurched under my feet, threatening to pitch me into the wash—but it was the last one, and it was just a short leap to the safety of the shore.

But taking the leap would mean abandoning the water. Turning my back on the stream, and the lands on the far shore. Setting my face forward. Knowing that this time, when I saw nothing there in front of me, it was not a case of a ghost who could hide behind thin air; that this time, for the first time, there really was nothing and nobody there, that I could look up into the sky through a veil of young leaves and catch the sparkles of sunlight dripping from the trees into the shade like a rain of diamonds, and see no face in the sky. No Lucy. Not anymore. I was free. So was she. I didn't have to turn around to know that the stepping stones had sunk without trace into the water that now ran deep above them. There was no going back.

Lonie reached out to touch my hand. "Are you all right? You look weird…"

"I'm fine," I said, and reached for the paper in her hand. "Give me that."

She held onto it for a moment. "What are you going to do with it?"

"I'll put it away with mine," I said. "Wherever I've got my copy of it. She's part of me. I'll file the paperwork where it belongs. But first...do you have a pen?"

She passed me the birth certificate, and reached up to the desk beside which she'd been sitting on the floor, rummaging around for a pen. She found one, and passed it to me; I took it and carefully inked in a name in the empty space that had been left on the certificate of birth.

A name for the nameless spirit. The thing she might have been waiting for all along.

Lucy.

I wrote her name down, and I saw her smile in the back of my mind, luminous, breaking the sky, spilling into other galaxies, a girl in whose eyes stars danced and glimmered, in whose hair a thousand suns shone. The second half of myself. The thing I had been missing all of my life without ever knowing that it had been lost. I held her to me, one more time. And then I let her go.

Alma Alexander's life so far has prepared her very well for her chosen career. She was born in a country which no longer exists on the maps, has lived and worked in seven countries on four continents (and in cyberspace!), has climbed mountains, dived in coral reefs, flown small planes, swum with dolphins, touched two-thousand-year-old tiles in a gate out of Babylon. She is a novelist, anthologist and short story writer who currently shares her life between the Pacific Northwest of the USA (where she lives with the obligatory two writer's cats) and the wonderful fantasy worlds of her own imagination.

Find out more about Alma and her books: on her website, www.AlmaAlexander.org; at Patreon, www.patreon.com/AlmaAlexander; and at all the usual social media sites.

About the story

A little while ago someone came up with the idea of an anthology which, for want of a better way to describe it, might have been summed up as "Alt-Beatles"— stories which were "what-if" stories concerning the Beatles themselves…except that the story that occurred to me was not about the Beatles, as such—it was about a song, "Lucy in the Sky with Diamonds." My alt-Beatles story flowered around THAT. The editors liked it but it wasn't quite right for their vision at the time— and so Lucy's ghost came back to me. I'm happy she found the *right* place to haunt at last.

Love in the Company of Ghosts

Steven Popkes

The living have God, priests, Jesus and money. All ghosts have is Mister Gray.

It was Mister Gray who convinced me I was dead after he found me sitting next to my dismembered corpse in 1935. I ran one of the few Worcester shoe factories that stayed open during the Great Depression and during a routine inspection had fallen into the leather shearing machine. The factory closed after that. A shadow on a shadow, as we say. There's no use in talking about one's life afterwards.

Mister Gray always wore a fedora and it gave his gray face a shadow of ambivalence: pity mixed with scorn, compassion with impatience. He counseled me as to moving on or staying here and the rules of post-mortem behavior when I decided to remain. He taught me how to maintain a form in daylight or evening or a stiff wind. How to show a face or a hand, to pluck a penny or crush a flower. How to be seen and not seen and who could see us despite our efforts—cats did but usually ignored us. Sometimes dogs. Rarely humans.

It was Mister Gray who persuaded me to join the

company and gave me my first journeyman gig in Providence—nameless tasks that every ghost must do before it can truly enter the business. Knocking on walls, opening doors, flushing toilets—all those anonymous special effects that give such verisimilitude to the main acts. It was Mister Gray who suggested I try out for a mansion haunt. "Jack," Mister Gray said. "You look every inch the businessman. You were made for the role." I was quite pleased.

There I met Amy.

Amy was lively and quick—everything I am not. She could paint her face cold and white as the moon and then warm it with a quick smile that positively glowed as if she were alive. Fingers, lips, faces, eyes— the features ghosts show to one another. The curve of cheek to chin, nose to mouth. I covertly watched Amy every chance I could. Sometimes not so covertly.

Belcourt Castle was a two-ghost act: two spirits connected to a wedding painting purchased by Oliver Belmont in 1899. They were seen spottily here and there in the castle but the finale was always an arm-in-arm promenade down the main staircase. Amy was pleased with the part since she'd been playing the Tiny Woman over at the old Wedderburn House—a part with limited range. I was pleased with her on my arm, once I had fully understood how to keep an arm intact.

"Mister Gray must have his eye on you," she said. "This is a sweet role."

I was instantly smitten.

Even so, after a while I grew bored with everything about the role save Amy. Merely walking about looking business-like grew tiresome. I yearned for something more interesting, something different from what I'd done in life.

I didn't tell Amy I had auditioned for the Hanging Man in the Chicago Water Tower. It was most definitely not business-like and Chicago was about as far from home as I'd ever been. When I told Amy she informed me she'd auditioned for the part of Resurrection Mary and would also be coming to Chicago. *Joy!* We weren't working *exactly* together but we were still able to haunt the same café when schedules permitted. I admitted my feelings for her and, to my grateful surprise, she said she felt the same.

Amy was a consummate professional. Resurrection Mary was a role with real fraternization. The haunt was expected to hold living conversations or even be able to touch a member of the audience—the sudden realization of death and mortality being the point of the act. To actually speak with the living as if I were still alive filled me with dread. Amy relished the prospect.

It was from Amy I learned most of my craft. In trying for the Hanging Man, I had considerably underestimated the role and overestimated my own talent. I had no idea what I was doing. Sure, I could walk down a stair in Newport looking like something I'd been in life: a businessman. But the Hanging Man had to evoke terror of life, an ultimate escape, a silent swinging act of protest, a demonstration of utter despair, a shameless act of self-gratification—all of these from a glimpse through a window across the street. It was Amy who steadied me, helped me explore the character and determine how to best show the depth the character deserved. When finally my act opened, it was entirely due to her efforts that I was ready.

We were married the following year, in the dead of winter just outside of the Shedd Aquarium. Mister Gray presided. He even smiled. Thinly, but I noticed.

I would have happily stayed in Chicago forever.

There were no shortage of roles and when we weren't haunting there were places to gather, ghosts to see—a continuing party in the Taxidermy Department of the Fields Museum and the annual Industrial Ball in the Museum of Science and Industry. The Christmas Underwater Lake Walk and the Chicago River Spring Cotillion. But Amy wanted to play the big time. She wanted to go to New York. If *she* wanted to go to New York, *I* wanted to go to New York.

So, it was in 1943, at the height of the war, Mister Gray sent us to New York. We were the Mayfair Hotel Couple, a husband-and-wife murder-suicide dated from 1910.

———◆———

I loved the Mayfair Hotel, from its postage stamp rooms to the shared bathrooms where the plumbing wailed like the damned. It had been built with grand ideas in mind but the war had belittled them like it belittled all things. Instead of the kings and queens of society, we had a parade of soldiers staying at the Mayfair for a nickel a day. Soldiers all took leave in New York for the same reason: economy. A man could take the subway or catch a show for nothing more than the wearing of his uniform.

The role required fraternization just like Resurrection Mary. At first, I stumbled and lost an arm or an eye, causing horror rather than reflection. But Amy was there to help. By the end of our first year, I could sit with a boy from Iowa and talk to him about how he felt about the flat fields of home and the canyons of the city without him ever realizing he was speaking with a ghost. Then, slip backstage and watch to observe how he reacted when told by the desk clerk or the maid. We always planned for knowledgeable staff to be nearby. It was part of the effect. They were good boys and a little reflection was good for their souls.

The war ended. We passed most of the fifties executing the precise pirouette of selecting the audience, presenting the act and withdrawing to determine the effect. The Mayfair was all unrehearsed improv, the artistic pinnacle of creating a moment of impact. I worked hard—improv was never easy for me. Until I had developed a repertoire of possible responses, I was never more than a wooden model of a man. Once I had learned enough to have something to fall back on when I was at a loss, I developed enough confidence to expand the role, to steer actual conversations instead of merely presenting stony anecdotes.

Amy had none of my issues. It came as naturally to her as breathing, had she any breath.

Toward the end of the Eisenhower administration, when hatted men wore gray flannel suits and women enjoyed the universal suffrage of the kitchen, the hotel changed from housing transient vacationers to a collection of permanent residents and a smattering of business travelers. A fire in their Queens house drove Dan and Lucy Sterling, a young couple in the south end of their twenties, into the Mayfair. They needed time to settle the insurance and determine if they would rebuild the house or find a new one. They needed a place to live and the Mayfair was close to where Dan worked. It was late autumn.

Lucy was all nervous action and wit, quick with a comment or tears, her emotions always showing as bright and obvious as a bird.

Dan looked like a baseball player, all rangy muscles and smooth energy. Blue eyes, dark hair, cheekbones like Lincoln's but without the homeliness. He was an attractive man and knew it. Some men are powered by nervous heat and others burn through life like charcoal. Dan seemed lit by a warm, banked fire.

The act's conversations were necessarily limited to single encounters. Sure, there were some repeated glimpses or glances of recognition between us and the staff or some of the permanent residents—this was necessary in order for the participant to be told who, or what, he'd been speaking with. But the effect of the act disappeared if the conversations were continued and rounded out into whole interactions, its impact lost in a haze of familiarity.

I had not made any contact with Dan or Lucy. Dan intimidated me—he was so confident I couldn't figure out how to approach him. He had no *room* for reflection. With Lucy my hesitance was more based on concern. Any more reflection in that little bird might make her spin apart from sheer centrifugal force. I let them alone. There were enough business travelers passing through the Mayfair to serve and, on those rare weeks when there was no available audience inside the Mayfair, Amy and I could still find a hapless pedestrian for a solo performance.

We occupied a rude and waterless walkup on one of the abandoned upper floors where the elevators did not reach. We didn't sleep, of course. And the furnishings made little difference except to serve as a prop for habits we still retained from living. From there we often moved to the roof, basking in the rain's light or listening to the howl of the moon—things denied the living. It was a good approximation of life.

But now Amy did not come to the roof as often as she used to. Or she was distracted and lost in her own thoughts. Or she picked a fight with me—we'd *never* fought before. I avoided conflict like the plague and

Amy was too much in control to let a fight happen. I was bewildered.

Then, she started neglecting the act.

Scheduled conversations were abandoned. Improv opportunities were skipped. Often, she was nowhere to be found. I was shocked—it was Amy who had taught me the law of the craft: the show must go on. It didn't matter whether or not you *felt* like it or if you were *up* for it or you would rather be somewhere *else*. The show *must* go on.

Mister Gray came to me as I was standing on the roof, wondering what was happening.

"Jack?" he said in his soft voice.

I turned to see him, pale face, gray hat, gray suit, gray tie all offset by the white, white shirt.

I nodded. "Hello."

He returned my nod and stood next to me, watching the roilings of the night. "I'm thinking of closing the Mayfair."

"You can't *do* that!" I cried. "It's a great show. We've been delivering for years. Haven't I—"

He looked at me and I dried up. Whatever was going on, he knew about it. Knew more than I did.

He looked back over the rooftops. The muted roar of Times Square seemed closer, seemed to come from him as he spoke.

"I'll give it a month," he said at last. "A month to pull the show together. That should be enough time."

He patted me on the shoulder—how long had it been since someone had done that? "You'll handle it. Right, Jack?"

I nodded miserably, feeling out of my depth as completely as I had back in Chicago. As I had in life.

He was gone when I looked up.

The first step was obvious. Amy and I had to talk.

I waited until Amy made an appearance in our flat.

She showed up walking through the door. I was sitting in the big upholstered chair—my affectation when I felt insecure. She saw me and showed a quick flash of panic. Then, her appearance steadied. Amy smiled at me. "Hey there."

I smiled uncertainly back. "Hello. Where have you been?"

"Oh, around."

"You missed a cue in the fourth-floor lounge."

She shrugged. "I didn't think the approach was right so I skipped him. He'll be here all week. There'll be a better opportunity when he's coming back from a sales call."

"Ah," I said. "And the cue yesterday? In the elevator?"

"I thought—"

"And the cue last week? Downstairs in the foyer?"

Amy stared at me. "What's this all about?"

"Mister Gray spoke to me this evening." I returned her stare. "He's thinking of closing the show."

"He can't *do* that! We've been—"

"One of us has."

She flared up at me. "You conceited little prick! How dare *you* lecture *me* about the craft?"

I didn't say anything for a moment. "Be that as it may. We have a month to pull the show together. If we don't, Mister Gray is closing us down. I don't know where we'll go after that."

She looked at me coldly. "*We* won't be going anywhere." And she vanished.

Well, I thought. That could have gone better.

Amy didn't come back to the flat. I didn't even see her except occasionally and she vanished when she noticed I was there. She abandoned the act altogether. I tried to pick up the slack, snatching improv opportunities that were beyond me and gamely trying to step up, taking her cues as well as my own. But it was clear the show was floundering.

I had to find out what Amy was doing, something neither easy nor obvious. How do you follow a ghost? Disappearance is our grace, our best effect, the leitmotif of our existence. If we didn't want to be found, we weren't found.

I eavesdropped on the serving staff to see if she was showing up to them. Nothing. The Mayfair had a cat, Roosevelt. I was desperate enough to try to talk to him but the cat ignored me until I prevented it from eating. Then, it snarled at me.

"What the fuck do *you* want?"

"I'm trying to find my wife. Amy."

"The other useless ghost." Roosevelt sat back and licked its chops. "None of my business. None of yours to mess with mine. Fuck off."

"What do you know?"

"I know enough not to bother *me* about it."

He started for his food again but I put my hand between him and the bowl.

Roosevelt reared back. Hissed at me. "You're thick. Fuck the food. Eat it and be sick." With that, Roosevelt stalked off.

Just as well. Cats are difficult at the best of times and lie continuously for no reason.

On the third floor lived the Campbell family. Their son, a young man named Jerry, was stricken with cerebral palsy. Every morning his father placed him in a chair in the hallway. During the day he was brought in, cleaned up, and placed back in the hallway by his mother. He was retrieved back into the apartment when his father returned from work. It was rough on him but being out in the hall he was able to watch people and pretend to participate. I had found him pleasant company.

"Hello, Jerry," I said as I appeared to him.

"Hi, Jack." His voice was thick and slurred, broad with his struggles with the intricacies of vowels. Being dead, I had no difficulty with it.

"Are you all right, honey?" Mrs. Campbell came out to check on him.

Jerry nodded, a stuttering movement more like a seizure than anything else.

"I wish she could understand me like you," said Jerry.

"Do you have to go to the bathroom?" Mrs. Campbell asked.

With great effort Jerry managed to shake his head slowly. Mrs. Campbell retreated back inside the apartment.

"I'm looking for my wife," I said. "Have you seen her?"

Jerry didn't say anything for a long time. "It's not my place, man. I'm not the right one to ask. You have to listen for the right sounds."

"You've been listening to that jazz station again."

"It don't mean a thing unless it's got that swing."

"You *do* know something."

"You be careful, man. She'll break your heart."

I returned to our flat and thought about it. I wasn't so thick not to realize that Roosevelt and Jerry had told me something important. What conversations had I missed?

I followed the staff again. This time with a more sensitive ear. Maybelle, the third-floor maid, gossiped with Buck, the chief bellhop, about how Lucy Sterling was beside herself. Dan wasn't coming home until late at night and there were fights. One of the cooks passed it on to the concierge, adding another nugget about the Sterlings: Lucy had made a snide comment to Dan in the elevator. I listened to the elevator boys on break. Dan had been frequenting the abandoned upper floors. I had a sick feeling I knew what was going on.

I followed Dan for an entire day. Out from the Mayfair, watching him from the ceiling on the subway as we went to work—to my surprise Dan Sterling worked for the city as a civil engineer. Followed him back to the Mayfair, up the elevator to his apartment and watched as he stood there, staring at the door, his keys in his hands.

Dan replaced the keys in his pocket and went to the stairwell. He walked up the next three floors, past where the elevators went, to the floor below ours. Then, he walked down the dust-covered hall to an apartment and opened the door. The door was unlocked. He opened it and went in, closed it after him. I stood outside.

This apartment was the flat below ours.

For a long time, I stood outside the door.

It was quiet in the hallway and I heard nothing from inside the apartment. Not that it mattered. I *knew* what was going on in there.

I could just leave, I thought. Leave the show. Leave the craft. Maybe even move on. Whatever happened after this could only be an improvement. Let Mister Gray handle things. Let him close down the show. Clear the Mayfair—clear New York for all I cared—of ghosts or anything else. Scour the place to earth and stone. Punish Amy for what she had done.

I thought a long time about what to do next.

In the end, there was nothing else to do. For good or ill—*especially* ill—I had to go in. This was the part I had to play.

The apartment was dark but I could hear them in a back bedroom. I moved toward the sound.

The bedroom was lit by a dirty window to the outside. There was just enough light to give a little color to the room. Amy was astride him, moving slowly forward and back, moaning softly. He gripped her thighs and gasped when she moaned, moving with her. She flushed with each movement, exchanging pallor for color. Neither of them noticed me, each completely absorbed with consuming the other.

I backed out of the room and stood outside. I would have covered my ears but that would have done nothing. Whatever silence I had perceived before was an artifact of my own willful ignorance. Now, knowing, I could have heard them from the moon.

Eventually, the sounds of activity ceased. Still, I waited. After perhaps an hour, I heard Dan moving in the other room. A moment later he emerged.

"There are consequences for such things," I said.

He jumped back, startled. "Who's there?"

I allowed myself to be seen. "I'm Jack. Amy's husband."

He collected himself and stood up straight. "I see."

"No, you don't." I stepped forward. He stepped back. "Tell me, *Dan*. Do you feel restless? Unfulfilled? What do you see when you look at people now? Are they contaminated with mortality? Do you see the death beneath the flesh?"

Dan stepped back. He raised a hand between us. "I don't know what you're talking about."

I followed him. "There's an *exchange*. I can see what she gets from you—no doubt you can see it, too. What are you getting from her?" I had never before conceived of a liaison between the living and the dead but I knew I was speaking the truth. The dead have instincts of their own.

"Get back."

"I'm her *husband*, Dan."

"You're dead."

"So is she, *Dan*. What difference does that make?"

"Leave him alone." Amy appeared next to me.

I looked at her, saw her graven face, cold, with only a residual flush on her cheeks and lips.

"As you wish," I said and left them.

⬥

Furious, I went downstairs to Dan and Lucy's apartment. I pulled myself together as best I could so that I looked as real and human as possible.

Lucy opened the door. "Yes?"

"My name is Jack Felton. I need to talk to you about Dan. May I come in?"

She nodded and I proceeded to enter, remembering to walk, to keep my feet on the floor and remain solid. This is not the act, I kept telling myself. I looked at my hands. They were not shaking. I was surprised.

"Please sit down," she said. "Did something happen to him? Is he all right?"

I sat on the sofa next to her. "Dan is having an affair with my wife."

She sat across from me. Her face crumpled and she cried. "I knew it," she said.

I realized how artfully she had made up her face as the tears ruined the effect. I had a sudden vision of her desperately trying to make herself more attractive, trying to keep her husband at home with her. She was pretty enough, I thought. She shouldn't have had to work at keeping him.

I reached out my hand and patted her shoulder and she clutched at me, pulled me to her. I felt awkward. Carefully, I held her. This was more contact with the living than I'd had since long before I had died. I tried to remember the motions of comfort. Oh, yes. I had to remain warm.

Then, she kissed me.

I was so startled I almost let myself go. But I kissed back, felt the first sluggish waves of life from her, tasted the salt of her tears, smelled the musk from her. Yes, I thought. Do to Dan what he had done to me. Do to Amy what she had done to me.

Do what Amy had done.

Gently, I separated myself from her. "No," I said. "Neither of us want that."

She pulled away and put her hands in her lap. "What am I going to do?"

"I don't know." I held her hand. I could still feel a suffused warmth from her. Nothing she couldn't spare or I couldn't handle. "Wait for him, maybe? This will not last. Such things can't."

"Is that what you're going to do?" She turned her blue eyes on me.

I realized I had made my choice. "Yes. It is."

<hr />

My choice, as little as it was, did not have much bearing on subsequent events.

The following day I was sitting in the shadows of our apartment when Amy appeared.

"What you did was inexcusable," she said in a hiss.

"Hardly."

"Following me, hounding me—"

"Finding my *wife* sleeping with another man."

"A *living* man," she said. "With flesh and blood parts and not a thin mockery—"

"Enough," said Mister Gray.

The living have God, priests, Jesus and money. All ghosts have is Mister Gray.

The gentle demeanor I had become accustomed to was gone. He looked dark and terrible, lit with black intensity. I felt afraid.

"Amy, you're fired," he said with a grim implacability.

I looked at her. She looked sunken, withered under Mister Gray's glare.

"All right," she said.

Mister Gray didn't speak for a moment. "I don't think you understand. I don't mean you're fired from the Mayfair. I mean you're fired from the company."

"What?" she asked, disbelieving. "From everything?"

"Everything."

"You can't mean that."

"Amy," he shouted at her. "You slept with a mortal. Now he can see us all. You're addicted and you've made him addicted as well. He can show others. It'll be *years* before I can undo the damage you've caused. *You endangered the company.*"

I could see it dawn on her. Dropped from the company, shunned by other ghosts, shouldered aside if she tried to create her own part, cast out to snatch at scraps: appearing in the corner of a glance, the edges of drug dreams, the borderlands of madness.

"*Please!*" she cried and fell to her knees. "Bit parts. Supporting cast. Script coach—*I can be a stage manager!* Something!"

"I wash my hands of you."

I couldn't stand it. "No."

Mister Gray turned to me, gaze frosty.

I stared back. "You fire her; you must fire me."

"Jack," he said softly. "You've done nothing wrong except choose poorly in love. I have no quarrel with you."

I looked at her, past my anger and hurt, past what she had done, to the Amy I had first met back in Newport. "She's my wife. If you cast her away, you must cast me away also."

He thought about it. I could see it cross his expression. He considered tossing us both. Mercy battled justice.

We were lucky. Mercy won.

"All right," he said. "But you're fired from the Mayfair. I'm closing that down."

"Thank you," she whispered.

He stared hard at Amy. "And if you consort with a mortal again—*any* mortal—I'll do more than fire you. I'll dissipate you." He saw her doubt. "Don't think I can't. Never forget I am in charge." He looked from one of us to the other. "But what to do with you now?"

Which is how we ended up with Ringling Brothers.

Like any addiction, one is never free. There is only an indefinite time between relapses. But Amy has been strong and I've been there when she wasn't. I wouldn't say our run at the Mayfair made the marriage better. But it is different and not all for the worse.

It's an extremely low-grade haunting—no visuals at all. We move things. A salt shaker put away in one trailer is found in another. Trapeze bars are found swinging of their own accord when the flyers come in to practice. Poltergeist sorts of things. Below even journeyman level.

The circus is filthy and the backstage thrill we enjoyed before is in short supply. Amy dwells too much on how far we have fallen and how hard we'll have to work to make a comeback—if we're able to make one at all.

But I console myself, and her, amidst the squalor.

At least it's show business.

Steven Popkes lives in Massachusetts on two acres where he and his wife raise bananas, persimmons, and turtles.

He works in aerospace making sure rockets continue to go where they are pointed. He insists he is not a rocket scientist.

He is a rocket engineer.

About the story

This story came, in part, from staying at this tiny Manhattan hotel years ago when the SFWA Author Publisher was still being held in New York. The rooms were tiny. The building was narrow. It struck me as a place with a history.

Then, later, I was thinking of classical haunting stories from the ghost point of view. Clearly, this had to be theater. What else could it be?

That's when the story started showing up.

House Is Where the Heart Is

Marissa Doyle

September 1923
London

"Ah, it's my dear Marie Louse! What a surprise, ma'am!"

I snorted at my dear friend Sir Edwin's use of my nickname and at his feigned astonishment at seeing me here at his house in Mansfield Street. We usually had tea on Thursdays to catch each other up on what we'd accomplished in the preceding week, though it hardly seemed necessary; I was in and out of his house almost constantly these days. But old habits died hard, and anyway, we enjoyed this ritual.

"Wait until you see what arrived today!" Sned rubbed his hands together gleefully as he stepped aside to let me in.

"Oh? What?" I followed him to the drawing room door, which was closed. "More books for the library?"

"No."

"The shipment of Bass Ale?"

"That came yesterday. Along with the towels for the Queen's bath."

"Oh, I must see those!"

"In a moment. You still haven't guessed today's arrival."

"I have to guess? Sned, you're a beast!"

Tea was already waiting for us on the few bits of furniture still left in the room. They were tucked away into a corner to make room for the project that filled the rest of the space—a project that had occupied Sir Edwin Lutyens, brilliant, celebrated architect and designer, and me, Princess Marie Louise, grand-daughter of Queen Victoria, cast-aside wife of Prince Aribert of Anhalt, and patroness of the arts, for the last two years.

Two years ago, with the Great War barely over, England was trying to return to a peacetime economy and I was trying to think of a way to acknowledge the enormous role Her Majesty the Queen Mary—also known as my dearest childhood friend, May—had played in our winning that war. She'd been a tower of strength for the king, my cousin George, doing an enormous amount of work in her quiet way to shore up the country's spirits. Everyone else got medals and honors and whatnot at the war's end, but she'd received nothing.

And then I had a brain wave that would help both efforts. May had always adored beautiful things, especially miniature ones, and that fact inspired me: wouldn't it be fun to present her with a re-creation of an elegant, comfortable English house, full of beautiful things yet with all the modern conveniences…but built on a one-inch-to-the-foot scale? A dolls' house, yes— but also a means to celebrate what we'd all fought to preserve: the best and loveliest of English art and culture, as produced by English craftsmen and manufacturers.

There was one other reason I was so taken with this idea, a personal one: I'd never had a house of my own. Aribert and I had never had one together; I'd spent the nine years of our marriage under my in-laws' roof, or traveling abroad alone when life with him became unbearable. This would be my chance—if a vicarious one—to satisfy my longing to nest.

I'd broached the idea to my old friend, Sir Edwin. He'd been charmed by it and agreed at once to design the house. I used my fat address book and, yes, my status as a member of the royal family, to cajole, corral, and coerce artists and businesses in every discipline to contribute to the project.

And my word, did they come through! Authors and composers wrote original works to be inscribed into tiny bound books for the library (well, apart from a few, like Mr. Elgar and Mr. George Bernard Shaw, who haughtily refused). Linens, from tablecloths to bed-sheets, were specially woven in Belfast and mono-grammed with tiny, perfect stitches. August members of the Royal Academy painted original artworks for the walls. The House had hot and cold running water, electric lighting, a tiny gramophone with records that played, a cellar full of vintage wines, and a fleet of motor-cars from Rolls-Royce that actually ran. The only thing we hadn't been able to include were working telephones.

The house had stood here in Sned's drawing room for two years (Lady Lutyens was a saint) while all the finish work and decoration took place. Workmen came and went, painting, installing, perfecting; but today, we were alone. I was glad for that; it would make dropping my bombshell on poor Sned a little easier.

Sned poured tea then brought over the new arrivals. I exclaimed over the tiny, perfect bottles of Bass' King's Ale for the wine cellar and stroked the embroidered towels with a reverent finger, and waited for Sned to finish drawing out his enjoyment of my impatience to see what else had arrived for the house.

Fortunately, his impatience to show me won: he placed a small wooden box on the table and reverently lifted the lid. There, nested in velvet, was a wee, perfect suit of armor.

"For the front hall! It came!" I nearly bounced on the sofa in excitement. "Can we put it in the house now?"

He pretended to frown at me. "Patience, patience! Mr. Jenkins will install it tomorrow and secure it properly in place. If you're very good, I'll let you be here to watch."

"Spoilsport," I said. But we were beaming at each other. There wasn't much left to do; in another few months, the ceremony presenting the house to Her Majesty would take place, just before it went to be shown at the British Empire Exhibition…which fact jogged my memory. Time was getting short, and if we were to add this last detail I'd thought of to the house, we would need to make haste.

I was trying to frame how to explain my idea when he spoke. "Out with it, my friend. You've been scowling into your teacup for the last five minutes. Is something the matter?"

"Yes." I took a deep breath. "There's something we've forgotten."

"For the house? How could there be? We've crossed every T and dotted every I, as far as I can see. There's lav paper in the loos and tea in the pantry. We've forgotten nothing."

"Actually, we have. Something very important."

It was his turn to (metaphorically) squirm with impatience. "What?"

"Well, I was reading a story by Saki last night," I began. "You must know the one—it's called 'The Open Window' and it's about a man paying a call at a country house who is terrified when the ghost of the missing owner suddenly reappears, and—"

Sir Edwin was watching me over his lifted teacup with every outward sign of patience, but I knew better. "—And that's when it occurred to me. Every English house worth its salt has a resident ghost. So must ours."

He set his cup in its saucer with enough firmness that I feared for its handle. "A ghost."

"Yes."

"As in clanking chains and headless women in black coaches and pale, gibbering revenants trailing tattered shrouds?"

"I should hope we could find one with a bit more of an aesthetic sense than that, but that's the general idea."

He regarded me in silence for a moment longer, then sighed and straightened in his seat. "I see. Do you have any notion where we might obtain such an item as a ghost? Fortnum's, perhaps? Hmm—will they have one in the correct scale?"

I wasn't sure if that was sarcasm or not; he was studiously avoiding my gaze. "Don't be silly. If ghosts can"—I waved my hands about—"ooze through keyholes and walk through walls and such, I should think one would be able to live quite happily in a dolls' house."

He took a sip of tea. "That does lead one to inquire about whom it is a ghost will be haunting."

Yes, definitely sarcasm. "Ghosts don't have to haunt anyone. Most of the time they just wander about minding their own business. A house without a ghost would feel—"

"Peaceful?" His eyes had begun to twinkle.

"Un-English!" I countered. "And you know what Her Majesty would think about that."

That made him laugh, and I knew I'd won. "Very

well then," he said. "But my question stands: where do we find a ghost?"

* * *

It was a good question. Where did one find a ghost?

My first thought was to contact Sir Oliver Lodge. Sir Oliver was a terribly clever scientist who, after his son was killed in the war, wrote books on ghosts and spirits and the survival of the mind after death. Surely he would have some ideas for us. Then Sned reminded me that Sir Arthur Conan Doyle, who had already contributed a book to the library, was also a spiritualist and might be willing to help us out. Both agreed enthusiastically to ask their fellow spiritualists and mediums about where we might find a ghost willing to move into the Queen's Dolls' House.

Curiously enough, though, none of these ladies (and a few gentlemen too, though it was mostly ladies) seemed to know how we should go about recruiting a ghost. I dutifully wrote to each medium Sir Oliver and Sir Arthur referred to me but only a couple replied, and they didn't hold out much hope for us.

"I don't know what we should do," I said to Sir Edwin a few weeks later, once again over tea. "My inquiries to the mediums have not been very successful."

"Ah. You've hit a dead end, I take it?"

"Sned!"

He gave his puckish grin. "I'm sorry. But you rather asked for that one."

"That doesn't mean you had to give in to the temptation. Anyway, it seems that mediums are not used to such requests. They are more concerned with helping those who have, ah, crossed the river—"

He harrumphed. I pretended not to have heard

him. "—and aiding them in moving on from this sphere rather than finding a new place to haunt."

"Good heavens."

"Yes, most of them seemed quite affronted at the idea."

"No, I was thinking about how geographical it all sounds. Rivers and spheres—perhaps we ought to consult an atlas."

That time, I laughed. "I don't think an atlas will be of much help. A few of the mediums—media?—did promise that they would let me know if anyone—er—thing came to mind."

"Kind of them," Sir Edwin said. "Hmm…where else does one go when trying to fill a position? I don't suppose an employment office would be of any use. I expect they prefer their clientele to be corporeal."

I knew he was pulling my leg again, but I was too dispirited to protest. "Yes, I expect so."

"Or…I know!" He sat up straighter. "We'll advertise! Let's see…" He narrowed his eyes and recited, "Situation available for a qualified individual…er, specter? Spook? Ectoplasmic person? to haunt a gentleman's residence. Experience preferred; knowledge of royal etiquette essential. Must be no more than seven inches tall. Room and board provided—no, scratch that, I don't suppose a ghost would require board—umm…room provided. Thursday afternoons and Sundays off, plus two weeks in August. References required. How's that?"

I sighed. "Will you be serious?"

"I am being serious. What's wrong with an advert? Of course, we'll have to be careful about which publications we place it in. *Country Life* and the *Times*, of course, but I would worry that if we place it in the wrong magazines, we won't get the class of ghost we're looking for."

I gave him my best stern look, learned at my grandmother's knee. "Oh, really, Sir Edwin!"

❖

The advert went out in *Country Life, Tatler,* both the daily and Sunday editions of the *Times,* the *Post,* and the *Mirror* as well as the *Guardian* and papers in Liverpool, Manchester, Edinburgh, and Glasgow. In addition, I sent it to a few country papers in Cornwall, Devon, and Wales.

"Why those?" Sir Edwin asked, pointing at the last three places when I showed him my list.

"They're reputed to be the most haunted areas of Britain."

"On whose authority?"

"Oh, everyone knows that, Sned." Actually, I hadn't until my lady-in-waiting, Evelyn, had told me, but he didn't have to know that.

"Hmmph. And the *Daily Mirror*? Really?"

"Don't be such a snob."

He put on an air of exaggerated patience. "I'm merely surprised that we didn't look for a more specific venue for the adverts. *The Graveyard Examiner* or the *Daily Crypt,* perhaps. I don't know if they do a Sunday edition, though."

I ignored that. "As a matter of fact," I said in as off-hand a manner as I could muster, "we've already received inquiries about the position."

"We have?" His astonishment was gratifying.

"Oh, yes. From the papers in North Wales and Devon."

"And?"

I thought about putting him off, but couldn't bring myself to. Finding a ghost to haunt the house was more important than my self-regard. "Unfortunately, the one from Devon was a spectral black dog—"

"A dog reads the local papers?"

"No, of course not. A group of—er, concerned local business owners on Dartmoor offered to convince it to relocate to the Dolls' House. It seems the dog's been frightening away holiday cottage renters."

Sned's moustache twitched. "And the Welsh spook?"

I sighed. "Spooks, actually. Seventeen miners killed in a colliery collapse. But they insist on being hired as a group, and I didn't think there was sufficient need to hire seventeen ghosts."

"My word." He shook his head. "Even the ghosts are unionizing. What are we coming to?"

I set down my cup. "Why do I get the impression that you're not taking this as seriously as you ought?"

His grin faded. "Well, really, how seriously should I be taking this? Hiring a ghost to haunt a dolls' house? My dear Marie Louse, this has been a delightful joke, but really, I think it's gone far enough. Shall we get back to work—real work—now?"

I picked up my purse and rose. "It's not a joke," I said, and swept out of the room.

Sir Edwin and I didn't talk for some days after that, while I let my bruised feelings soothe themselves. Really, how could I expect him to know anything about ghosts? He was an architect, after all: his preoccupation was with new buildings, no matter how much their style was an outgrowth of the past. He hadn't grown up in Windsor as I had, which was so steeped in a thousand years of history that it was a wonder the ghosts didn't outnumber the living.

Nevertheless, his attitude hurt. Perhaps my desire

to find a ghost for the house had become a little bit of an idée fixe. But I wanted the Queen's Dolls' House to be perfect in every way: May deserved nothing less. Why shouldn't it have a ghost if we could find one? If Sir Edwin chose to think it was nonsense, then I would simply have to show him otherwise.

Or so I told myself in my more confident moments.

The problem was how to show him; evidently, the ghosts of England were not keen on new employment opportunities. I did have a few more responses to my adverts, but only one was serious—and, it turned out, was from a poltergeist with decidedly republican leanings. Although I tried very hard not to be an elitist, even I had to draw the line somewhere.

In the meanwhile, a family wedding was occupying whatever dregs of attention I had left over from the Queen's Dolls' House: my young cousin Maud was marrying Lord Carnegie. I did love weddings; having the chance to catch up with family members I didn't often see was lovely—and we were a rather large family. But they also made me melancholy. I was invariably reminded of my own wedding, when I was nineteen and head over heels in love with my handsome bridegroom. I prayed that a merciful God would not let dear Maud find herself like me, trapped in a loveless marriage and eventually discarded by her husband and his family after nine unhappy years. But if she did, we would rally around her, just as my grandmother and the rest of my family had for me. What would any of us do without people who care for us?

Just a few days after Maud's wedding, Sned telephoned me. I put on my most gracious tone when my lady-in-waiting handed me the receiver. "Sir Edwin, it's a pleasure to talk to you! How are you? How is Lady Lutyens?"

He ignored my effusions. "How quickly can you get here?"

That startled me. "What, today?"

"Now, if it's possible."

I glanced at my watch. I was supposed to be lunching with the Queen at one so that we could have a good gossip about the wedding. It was barely nine. If I were careful, I could just make it to the Lutyens' house and back in time to dress for lunch—assuming that he wasn't summoning me to help mop up a disaster. "Why, yes, I suppose I can. But what is it? Is there anything wrong?"

Silence. Then, "I'd rather not say just now. Will you please come?"

Evelyn managed to hail me a cab in record time, and I arrived in Mansfield Street not much more than a half-hour after Sir Edwin's cryptic summons. He met me in the front hall, coatless and looking more than a little shell-shocked, and I forgave him on the spot.

"Thank God you're here," he said.

"I came as quickly as I could." In the cab ride over I'd begun to make a mental list of every possible calamity that he might not have wished to discuss over the telephone. "Please, tell me what has happened? Are you ill? Has something happened to the House?"

He opened his mouth to speak, then hesitated. "It's easier to just show you."

I followed him into the drawing room, which was still (thank goodness!) dominated by the great bulk of the Dolls' House, almost twice its actual height as the outer façade was raised above it by a winch attached to the ceiling (did I say just how saintly Lady Lutyens was?). Three or four of our most trusted workmen were huddled at one end of the room, all staring fixedly at the front of the House.

There, on the step leading to the House's front walk, was...well, I didn't know what it was. A small figure—very small—sat with his knees drawn up to his grizzled beard and his shoulders hunched, staring at me from under beetling brows. He clutched a tatty bundle to his chest, and his clothes—including an oddly pointed, battered red hat—were equally disreputable.

"Who're you?" he demanded, in a surprisingly deep voice for one so small.

"She's the person in charge around here, not to mention a princess, and you have precisely five seconds to stand up and remove your hat like a gentleman," Sir Edwin said sternly.

The little man cackled. "But I ain't a gennalman. And us gnomes don't take our hats off for no one. 'Sgainst our religion," he added. "B'sides, bare heads ain't healthy when yer out of doors as much as we are." But he did climb to his feet. His disproportionately large boots were patched at the toes.

I realized my mouth was hanging open and closed it. A gnome—he must be a garden gnome! "Er, how do you do, Mr.—?"

"Ain't no mister. Nor yet a missus." He chuckled at his own humor. "Gnomes don't go in fer handles like that. Name's Charg. Jus' Charg."

"I see," I said. Then, because he was looking at me expectantly, I added, "Well, Mr.—ah, Charg. Perhaps I've been mistaken, but I somehow thought gnomes were a little...taller."

He scowled. "So I was the runt o' the litter, wasn't I? Ain't none of your business, no how. An' it says in the paper you was wanting someone no more 'n seven inches. I'm seven 'n three-quarters, but I kin, you know, stoop. Like this." He drew his head further in until he looked like a hunchback and peered up at me sideways.

In the paper... "You're applying for the ghost position?"

"Why, you got any other jobs open?"

"But—ahem—" There really was no delicate way to say it, so I forged ahead. "Well, it's just that you're not particularly dead, as far as I can see. Ghosts usually are."

"Don't see why they hafta be, if they look the part. See, I brought m'own uniform." He held up the bundle he'd been clutching and shook it out. It was revealed to be a very grubby lady's handkerchief, with unraveling cheap lace trim around the hem. He draped it over his head, shifting it around until two badly-cut eyeholes were properly positioned. "There! How's that?"

Sir Edwin made a peculiar choking sound, quickly muffled. I shot him a sideways glare, but he was assiduously applying his own handkerchief in a more conventional manner to his nose, so I couldn't in good conscience accuse him of laughing. "That's...very creative, Charg."

He yanked it off and beamed at me. "So do I got the job?"

Sir Edwin stepped forward then and took my arm. "Might we have a word, please?"

"Excuse us," I said to Charg, and let Sir Edwin steer me into the corner. "I see the reason for the urgent summons," I said.

He wasn't laughing anymore. "How do you think I felt this morning when I came into the room after breakfast and found him sitting there, calm as you please? I haven't the faintest idea how he even got in."

"How did you think ghosts were going to get in?"

"I wasn't expecting any to actually show up! I thought this ghost search business was just a wheeze on your part."

I frowned at him. "How could you think that,

Sned? I've been very serious about every aspect of the Dolls' House from the start. You know how important it is to me."

He reached up and rumpled his hair with both hands. "But a ghost? And now this—thing? What are we supposed to do with it...er, him?"

I sighed. "I don't know. He's the only actual applicant we've had, aside from the poltergeist."

Sned blanched. "That wasn't a joke either?"

"Not at all." I looked over at Charg. He was loitering against one of the stone pillars of the front gate, bundling his ghost "uniform" over one arm and very carefully not looking at us. But something about the set of his head and shoulders told me that his nonchalance was far from genuine. For whatever reason, he very much wanted this job. I wondered why.

"Well." Sned gave himself a little shake and became quite business-like. "I appreciate his interest in the position, but no matter his, ah, dimensional qualifications—if he remembers to stoop, of course—the fact remains that he's not actually a ghost. We've been so very careful to be as authentic as possible in every other aspect of the House that I don't think we should relax our standards now."

I continued to watch Charg not watching us. "Yes, you're probably right."

"Well, that settles that. We'll tell the little blighter to go away."

"No," I said. I'm not sure who was more surprised—Sned or me.

Sned, bless him, kept his patience. "I thought we just agreed that he's not authentic and therefore unqualified?"

"Let's—let's at least give him a chance," I said quickly, before I could stop myself from being such a pushover. "He may not be a ghost but he must have some supernatural abilities if he managed to get in here without anyone noticing."

"Being seven—pardon me, seven and three-quarters inches tall might have helped with that," he said dryly.

"Perhaps," I admitted. "But even so—it wouldn't bring about the end of the world to let him try it for one day."

"Let's hope not," Sned said.

Charg was all business when we told him that we would give him a day's trial employment. "Will I get paid?" he asked suspiciously.

"Absolutely," I said, treading lightly on Sned's foot before he could speak.

"Shake on it, then."

I held out my hand. He grasped the end of one of my fingers and gave it a firm jerk. "Right. What's next?" He shook out his "uniform" and prepared to don it.

I could see Sned was about to deliver a sarcastic response and jumped in before he could. "Why don't I give you a tour of the House first, and we can talk about our expectations."

"Whatever they are," Sned muttered. I ignored him.

Giving a tour of a building you're not physically able to fit into is an odd experience. I found myself wishing I could see it all through his eyes, could have the experience of walking through it in its own scale. We had worked so hard to get it precisely right; how well had we succeeded?

I directed him down to the barrel-vaulted cellar level first to see the garage and the fleet of six automobiles. Charg wandered through the bays, pausing to run a hand longingly along the front fender of the Rolls-Royce limousine. "Does it run like a real one?"

"Yes. But don't get any ideas, please."

He sighed and I caught a muttered "spoilsport" which I pretended not to hear. "And over there's the wine cellar."

Even from where I stood, I could see his eyes grow round as he surveyed the bins full of bottles of vintage wine, the casks of beer and Scotch whisky, the shelves of spirits.

"No ideas about that, either, you," Sir Edwin called. I hadn't realized he was standing behind me.

Charg looked like he would like to reply to that, so I quickly said, "Sned, don't let us keep you. I can manage the tour myself if you're busy."

He took the hint and went over to confer with the workmen, but not before giving me a Look. I gave him my widest smile in return and went back to showing Charg around—past the dry goods stores then up the stairs to the ground floor. The kitchen and the dining room didn't seem to impress him much, but I noticed how he lingered in the library, looking at the shelves of books. "Those books there," he commented. "They're real too, like the booze downstairs?"

"All of them," I confirmed.

"Hmm."

I directed him up the stairs to the first floor, through the saloon where a pair of thrones dominated the room (he did not try to sit on them, but regarded them thoughtfully), through the Queen's bedroom, and into the King's. With each room he grew quieter, till even his incessant muttering under his breath, which had seemed more a function of breathing than actual words, ceased.

Next I sent him up the back stairs to the mezzanine, where the servants' bedrooms were, and then the top floor, where the day and night nurseries were. Charg crouched to look at the toy train set, the tiny dolls' house, the hobbyhorse, the toy stage, then rose, shaking his head.

"What is it, Charg?" I asked.

He hunched his shoulders. "I dunno. It's...I just ain't ever seen nothing like this before. A house full of stuff just like you big people have, but it's my size. I ain't never...you know...belonged nowhere. I was too liddle to be any good as a garden gnome, so me dad chucked me out when I was a big lad, and I ain't had nowhere that's home since. This is the first place I ever seen that fits me. Not that it really fits the likes o' me—them thrones..." He shook his head. "But here I could, like, sit inna chair"—he sat in the wingback chair by the nursery fireplace—"an' pick up a book or summat and set and read for a bit—so long as the words aren't too big," he added quickly. "Or sit at a proper table to have my tea, or sleep inna proper bed. Jes' one of them beds in the servants' rooms—don't have to be like the king's bed or nothing." He rubbed his nose reflectively. "This is a *home*."

Oh. I had to look away for a moment so that no one could see my face. So this was why he was so interested in the position here. Could I blame him, when I knew a thing or two myself about being "chucked out" and losing what I thought was my home, back in Anhalt?

Still, he was here to apply for employment as the House's ghost. I couldn't let myself forget that, despite my fellow feeling for him. "I'm glad you think so," I said more briskly than I felt. "A great many people have worked to make it seem like one. Now, about haunting it—"

"Oh, don't you worry none about that, mum. I got it covered." He patted the handkerchief draped over his arm. "I'll do my ghosting good and proper. You'll see."

I looked at my watch. "Actually, I'm afraid I won't. I have a luncheon appointment, but I'll come back at the end of the day and see how you've done. Sir Edwin will be here if you have any questions and to see how you do."

Charg stuck out his chest and threw out a salute with the wrong hand. "Yes, mum!"

Sned did not look delighted when I told him that I had to leave to get dressed for a luncheon. "Can't you beg off?"

"I would, if the invitation hadn't been from the Queen."

"Oh," he said glumly. "No piking off that."

"I promise I'll come back when it's over. She always sends a car for me, and I'll have it drop me here straight from the palace. But I'm sure everything will work out fine. I feel it in my bones."

He glanced over at the house. Charg could be seen before one of the looking glasses in the entrance hall, adjusting his uniform. The lace on the trim had caught on something, and a long thread trailed behind him. "Well, my bones would like to offer yours odds on that."

"Pish," I said. "I'll be back later."

I had a delightful time with May, rehashing Maud's wedding and discussing how much older everyone in the family was looking, aside from us. George had an engagement elsewhere so we were able to be quite merry—just like our girlhood selves—over our fricasseed chicken and ice cream with spiced peaches. She even sneaked one of my cigarettes after luncheon; George did not like to see her smoke.

"By the way, how is the Dolls' House progressing?" she asked, pouring us coffee.

"Splendidly!" I said. "We're right on schedule, with just a few last-minute items to come in and a few details to finish. I even have a surprise for you."

"A surprise?" Her eyes sparkled. "Lousie, you're a dreadful tease. What kind of surprise?"

"The perfect finishing touch. You'll see. It will probably be settled by this afternoon," I said confidently.

I should have listened to Sned's bones.

———————◆———————

As I'd promised, I asked the driver bringing me home to drop me in Mansfield Street instead. I was a little later than I'd told Sned I would be, but not egregiously so. Or so I thought.

"Where have you been?" he demanded, popping into the hall after the butler had let me in and helped me off with my coat. I opened my mouth to give him the obvious answer, but he'd already clamped onto my elbow to draw me toward the drawing room. We stopped just outside the door. "You hired the little menace," he muttered. "You get to fire him."

My heart sank. "What happened?"

"What didn't happen? For one thing, practically no work got done today because everyone in the room was too busy guffawing at what our new ghost thought constituted appropriately ghostly behavior."

"I suppose ghostliness is, er, in the eye of the beholder—"

"Not when the ghost in question makes noises like a sheep with a gut-ache."

"Oh, really, Sned. How do you know what a sheep with a gut-ache sounds like?"

"That's not the point. The point is that he sounded ridiculous. He spent a solid two hours marching—by thunder, he has a heavy tread for someone his size—through every room in a strict pattern, doing his sheep-in-gastric-distress cry every ten seconds. After a while it stopped being funny and just became annoying."

"You should have said something to him."

"I did. I told him to ruddy well stop it and do something else."

"Did he?"

"Yes. He waited until the workmen went back to work on the dry goods stores—they were unpacking and installing some cans we just received—and kept jumping out from behind the archway and shouting 'boo!' at them."

My sinking heart was now somewhere about my ankles. "To be fair, we didn't explain exactly what our expectations were—"

He held up a hand. "I'm not through yet. We told him in no uncertain terms that his presence was not required in the cellars, so he stomped back up the stairs doing his sheep cry again—the main staircase, mind you, not the back stairs—and into the King's Wardrobe, where that blasted 'uniform' of his caught the table there and pulled it over. Whereupon he himself tripped and fell, swearing like a navvy."

Oh, poor Charg! "He wasn't hurt, was he?"

Sned glared at me. "No, nor was the table."

"The table—yes, of course. I'm so glad," I said weakly. "What then?"

"I told him to take the damned hanky off and go sit outside where he couldn't hurt anything. He has to go," he said, more quietly. "You understand that, don't you?"

I understood, even if I didn't like it. "Where is he?"

"On the steps by the front door." He looked at me for a moment, then reached into his coat pocket for his wallet, from which he extracted a five-pound note. "His wages, plus severance."

I nodded and took the note, though I couldn't help wondering just what a seven and three-quarter-inch-tall gnome would do with it. Then I straightened my back and went in to sack our unsuccessful ghost.

Charg was on the steps where he'd been this morning, so sunk in gloom that he didn't notice me approaching until I stood before him. He scrambled to his feet as I pulled over a side chair. "Yer here to give me th' boot," he said flatly.

There didn't seen to be any good way to soften the blow. "I'm afraid so."

"Knew it." He sighed gustily and sat down again. "Is it a'cos I lied?"

"Why, what did you lie about?"

He looked down at his feet, but not before I caught the flush on his cheeks. "I'm not really seven an' three-quarters inches. I'm just seven—well, six and seven-eighths. Thought you'd all respeck me more if I was taller."

I found myself blinking back tears. "No, Charg, it wasn't that. It—it's mostly that we've tried very hard to be as authentic as possible with the Dolls' House and everything in it. You've had a chance to see that your-self—"

"And I ain't an authentic ghost," he finished.

"No."

"I tried. I really did." He sounded almost pleading. "I did what ghosts 'r supposed to do, didn't I?"

"Perhaps you tried a little too hard," I said, as gently as I could. "There are things that ghosts can do that a living body can't. We can't have you damaging the house in the process of haunting it."

"No, I s'pose not." He slumped back onto the step.

We sat in silence for a moment, contemplating our hands in our laps so that we wouldn't have to look at each other, until I gave myself a mental shake. "I have your wages for the day, plus a bit more—er—in lieu of notice." I added a banknote of my own to Sned's, hesitated, then rolled them up together tightly in a scroll and handed them to Charg. He took them in silence.

"What will you do now?" I put a heartiness into my voice that sounded false even in my ears. "Visit family, perhaps."

He looked at me. "Don't got any. They're gone."

Don't got any. I caught my breath as those three small words hit me with all the force of bullets. "I'm sorry, Charg," I finally said. "I can't imagine living without family. But their garden—your people were garden gnomes—"

"It ain't there no more. House got knocked down and the garden paved over. An' anyway, I can't abide gardens. Plants make me itch and sneeze, and I make 'em die." He shrugged. "That's part o' why me dad kicked me out when I was a lad."

A garden gnome who was allergic to gardens. Life could be so cruel at times. "So where will you go?"

"Dunno." He shrugged. "Back to wanderin' again. Ain't nothin' else fer me to do."

He looked at the notes rolled up in his hand like a pirate's treasure map, and held them out to me. "Thankee for these, mum, but there ain't much I kin do with 'em."

I couldn't bring myself to take them back. My darling mother, whom we'd lost just this June, had been the patron of a dozen charities that helped people help themselves; I could practically feel her prodding me in the shoulder, exhorting me to do something for poor

Charg. "No, you hold onto them," I said, and stood up. "We'll find something for you to do. I promise."

He regarded me dubiously. "If there's anyplace for th' likes o' me out there, I ain't found it yet."

"Let me sleep on it and we'll talk tomorrow. I'm very good at figuring things out. Oh, Sir Edwin," I called. "Charg will be staying here for the night."

"What, in the House?" Charg jumped up, his face alight.

Sned hurried over. "What, in the House?" His face emphatically did not light up.

"Just for the night," I said. "In the Butler's Room, I think. Good night, Charg. We'll meet tomorrow morning and figure out what your next step will be."

He looked up at me. The elation that had briefly illuminated his features had faded, but he tried to muster a smile. "Thank 'ee, mum. It'll be somethin', at least, to stay here fer a night."

"That's the spirit!" I gave him what I hoped was a confident nod, even as Sned seized my arm and marched me out of the room.

"Have you lost your mind?" he demanded, shutting the door behind him. "We just sacked him, and now you're inviting him to stay on as a guest?"

"It's just for one night," I said. "The poor thing has nowhere else to go."

"You could invite him to stay at your house."

"It wouldn't be the same. Oh, Sned, it was too awful. He tried to be a good ghost, as far as he was able—he really did. And he's fallen in love with the House, which makes it even worse."

He shook his head. "Then was letting him stay the night actually doing him a kindness?"

I tried to answer, but the lump in my throat wouldn't let me.

I arrived back in Mansfield Street bright and early the next morning, armed with a list of suggestions for Charg that was shorter than I'd hoped. But maybe one of my ideas would inspire him—at least, that was what I was counting on.

To my surprise, Sned himself answered the door. "You're early," he said, letting me in.

"I wanted to make sure Charg knows that I'm serious about helping him," I said, then noticed the saucer in his hand. "I'm sorry—did I disturb your breakfast?"

He cleared his throat, moving ahead of me to open the drawing room doors. "No, I—ahem…I was just about to bring Charg a bit of toast and a rasher of bacon."

"You old softie, you," I murmured, following him in.

He ignored me. "Hullo, Charg. Princess Marie Louise is here and we've brought you a spot of breakfast. Rise and shine, old man." He put down the saucer and went to the winch to raise the House's shell. "Stand clear—I'm raising the top."

There was no response.

"He's a heavy sleeper," Sned observed. He hoisted the shell and fastened the safety. One of the wheels of the winch mechanism squealed hideously.

"He may be a heavy sleeper, but no one could sleep through that," I replied, pulling off my gloves. "Good morning, Charg."

Silence.

Sned and I looked at each other, and almost as one hurried over to the other side of the House, where the Butler's Room was.

Charg was not there. But the bed had clearly been

slept in: the covers were thrown back and the pillows askew. A familiar-looking pair of worn work boots with patched toes was tucked neatly beneath it...and lying on the floor next to it were at least half a dozen small bottles.

Sned reached in and gingerly picked one up, less than an inch tall. "Bass' King's Ale," he read aloud, and looked up at me.

"Oh, Charg," I murmured. He had evidently decided to try to drown his sorrows, courtesy of the House's cellars. While I was disappointed, I couldn't find it in me to blame him. He had lasted barely a day in a job he'd very clearly wanted. He probably hadn't believed I sincerely wanted to help him find a more suitable place; when had anyone tried to help him? Besides, bottles of ale in just his size must have been an enormous temptation. "Where do you suppose he is? He can't have gone far without his boots."

Sned was already around the side of the House. "Oh," he said, stopping short.

"What is it?"

I was just behind him, but he held out a hand to stop me. "No, Louse—you don't need to see this," he said gently.

But I'd already guessed what he didn't want me to see, and I was right. Charg sprawled at the bottom of the cellar stairs, once again swathed in his "uniform"— a dangling thread of which entangled his stockinged feet. Even from where I stood I could see, under the thin cotton of the handkerchief, that his head was cocked at an unnatural angle. More bottles of ale lay scattered around him. One was broken, leaving a quarter-teaspoon-sized puddle on the stone floor.

My first thought was to try to take his pulse, but I quickly realized there was little point. I must have made some kind of sound, for Sned was right there, a reassuring hand on my shoulder. We gazed sadly at the little gnome's lifeless form.

Sned was the first to stir. "Why was he wearing that thing?"

"I don't know. Maybe he thought that because we let him stay here last night, he was still on duty."

He swallowed hard. "Do we know of any next of kin? Ought we to call the police to report an accidental death?"

"No family that I know of." I remembered Charg's flat tone as he told me how his father had kicked him out. "And what will the police do with a garden gnome who obviously fell down the stairs and broke his neck while inebriated? They'll probably accuse us of staging the whole thing for promotional purposes."

He sighed. "I expect you're right. We'll still have to, er, dispose of the remains somehow."

"We'll bury him in the garden—no, wait, he disliked gardens. Maybe I could sneak him into the Royal Mausoleum at Frogmore—I expect May could arrange it, if I asked. He would have liked that." I sighed too. "Poor Charg."

We stood for a moment, not saying anything. What could we say?

"At—at least he went out in style," I finally said. "In a house just his size, getting potted on Bass' King's Ale by the bottle. Not bad for an ex-garden gnome."

Sned pulled out his handkerchief. I was surprised for a moment—had Charg's sad death affected him more than I'd thought? But he was reaching into the cellar. "We ought to clean up before any of the workmen arrive," he said. "There's a box over by the table we can put him in—"

Just then, a small, very localized cold breeze caught at his handkerchief, fluttering it out of his hand. "What the devil!" he exclaimed, snatching at it.

But the breeze twitched it out of his grasp and puffed it a few feet away. Sned and I watched it fall slowly to the floor, perfectly billowed like a miniature parachute. An idea had formed in my mind, but I couldn't quite bring myself to believe what I was thinking...until a low chuckle behind us made us whirl round to face the house. A small, misty something hovered by the front gate.

"Well?" said a hollow voice—a ghost of a voice— that I was sure I knew. "It ain't what I planned, but is this authentic enough fer ye? Now kin I have the job?"

Marissa Doyle graduated from Bryn Mawr College and went on to graduate school intending to be an archaeologist but somehow got distracted. Eventually she figured out what she was *really* supposed to be doing and started writing. She's channeled her inner history geekiness into a successful young adult historical fantasy series, the Leland Sisters—*Bewitching Season, Betraying Season, Courtship and Curses* (all from Holt Books for Young Readers), *Charles Bewitched*, and *The Midwinter Hunt* (forthcoming)—and is now also happily writing fantasy of various types for teens and adults, including the just-released *What Lies Beneath*, also from Book View Café. She lives in her native Massachusetts with her family, including a bossy but adorable pet rabbit, and loves gardening, quilting, and collecting antiques. She has recently changed her morning beverage allegiance from coffee to tea, and was pleased to notice that the world has continued unabated to spin on its axis. Please visit her at her website, https://www.marissadoyle.com, and at her history blog, https://www.nineteenteen.com.

About the story

"House Is Where the Heart Is" was born when I was on a trip to England with my family in 2015. We were traveling with a family member who'd lived near Windsor for a few years, and while she went to see friends there one afternoon, we decided to spend the afternoon on a tour of Windsor Castle.

It was a wonderful tour: as it was close to the 200th anniversary of the Battle of Waterloo, there was a jaw-dropping exhibit of documentary material from the Windsor archives relating to the Napoleonic Wars, including things like Napoleon's hand-written letter of surrender to the Prince Regent. After my family dragged me away from that (yes, as a matter of fact I *am* a history nerd), and we'd seen the rooms on view to the public (also quite wonderful), we saw the signs for the Queen's Dolls' House. I'd forgotten it was kept at Windsor; I'd read about it and thought it might be fun to see it (and anyway, we had an hour to kill before meeting the aforementioned family member), so we got into the queue to view it.

Much to my relief, my family was charmed by it. The detail is exquisite: everything is *absolutely* to scale (I mean, fabrics specially woven for the upholstery and curtains so that their patterns would be correctly proportionate? The fully articulated suit of armor in the front hall? The garage with functioning cars and a motorcycle?) so it truly looks like a real house that just happens to be inhabited by very small people. Its creators wanted it to be an exemplar of a "perfect English house", we read on one of the descriptive placards; I turned to one of my daughters and said, "I wonder if it's haunted by a tiny ghost? Aren't all English stately homes haunted?" We laughed, but that idea stuck in my head...and here you are.

Special thanks are due to my nephew, from whose oft-recurring D&D character (a dwarf with a very high blood alcohol content) I borrowed the name "Charg."

La Dame Blanche

Brenda W. Clough

When I surveyed the house party at the Chateau de Séntillac, I could not forbear a comment. "Dearest Mignonne, what have you been thinking? Four gentlemen, and only we two ladies?" In French, of course, because I am fluent.

My friend and hostess, Marie-Louise, Marquise de Saint-Foi, smiled over the edge of her fan. "Do I not know it, *ma chèrie*? At school in Paris, did they not insist to us that for the gracious entertaining, the numbers must be equal? Ah, Marian, those were the days. The pranks we played! Do you remember when we stole the cabbages and used them for bowling balls? With wine bottles for the ninepins." Her large dark eyes, rimmed with black lashes, twinkled wickedly.

I laughed at the memory. "And when I jiggered the candles to mysteriously go out. A hot skewer severs the wick halfway along."

"And then you told the younger girls the tale of Anne Boleyn, the queen executed for adultery. Brr! Her restless spectre, carrying her own head down the corridors, a shuddersome tale. How Clothilde shrieked, when the candles went dim! But my Henri is in Paris on

business. We are women of years, and must be enter-
tained, and so I invite the young gentlemen. And your
stepson, the young Micah Camlet—sapphire-blue eyes?
I swoon! I had feared all Englishmen were unpre-
possessing. M. Hare, what a disappointment."

Mignonne has altered. At school we became
friends because we both had been adventurous to a
fault, but she had not been a shocking coquette. In
justice, however, I had to admit her point. The other
Englishman, Mr. Augustus Hare, was dovelike, slight
and soft-spoken, with a thin dark beard. One of those
young men of breeding but no wealth, he could smell
out useful acquaintance with the predatory instinct of a
wolf. Fortunately, his grasp of French is not good.

"Think of it, Mr. Camlet," he was saying to Micah
in English. "We are resident here in a chateau haunted
by a ghost! What if I spend the night in the haunted
chamber, eh? Should not my first-person account of the
adventure thrill the readers of your periodical?"

Micah has not been the editor of *Gadsbee's
Gallimaufry* for long, but he has already learned caution.
"What else do you write, Mr. Hare?"

"Guidebooks, sir. So far, Buckinghamshire, and
Durham. Do you know the story, Mrs. Camlet? So
tragical and romantic! It seems that the lord of Séntillac
went to the Crusades, leaving his wife Simone here.
Returning unexpectedly, he found that she was—
ahem." Mr. Hare rolled dark eyes in our direction.

The marquise only flirted her fan, but I replied,
"Caught *en flagrante*, I am to assume. An old story."

"Indeed, Mrs. Camlet. Indeed! In his fury her
husband the count walled her up in the tower room. For
the remainder of her life. And she haunts it to this very
day, am I not right, my lady? La Dame Blanche de
Séntillac! Shall you permit me to see the chamber?"

"Yes, the most thrilling tale," Mignonne said, in

her charmingly accented English. "Every historical chateau should have a ghost, eh? But the ancient tower has not yet been restored. What a deal of work we have before us, to rebuild all the walls and fortifications! If you ascend, you must climb up with care, M. Camlet."

"Not I," Micah replied. "I can't undertake to do more than look at your article, Mr. Hare. My father is the executive editor and reserves the final decisions for himself." This in fact was a slight exaggeration. My dear husband Theo still supervises the books and the pamphlet publications, but Micah founded the periodical and manages it. However, I made no comment. Publishing is not a field noted for its veracity.

"Then you must permit me to show you the new wing," Mignonne immediately said. "Henri has spent thousands of francs on it! And you, M. LeGrand, you must take my other arm."

She marshalled the selected swains and swept out in an opulent rustle of *tan d'or* silk and crinoline. The unfortunate Mr. Hare looked so crestfallen that I said, "Do you know, I've mistaken living persons for ghosts, once or twice. But never have I seen a genuine one, Mr. Hare. Have you?"

"My dear Mrs. Camlet," he immediately replied. "The number of stories I could tell you, about eerie happenings and haunted houses! And each of them recounted to me by persons of your quality and blood. Perhaps, since it is daylight, you would care to accompany me and look at the haunted chamber here?"

Something of a snob, our Mr. Hare—where does Mignonne find these people? "That would be mere foresight," I noted, "if you indeed mean to spend the night in it. As our hostess complains, most of the chateau is not yet habitable. You would wish to know if you need to bring your overcoat and an umbrella."

The drawing room we sat in was modern and

comfortable, part of the new ell. The surrounding citadel ramparts were merely heaps of tumbled yellow stone block. The chateau had been built high on a crag to defend the Dordogne against invaders in the twelfth century. So far as I could determine as we descended to the courtyard, not a franc had been spent on maintaining it since then. Mignonne, and her enormous dowry, must have struck Henri as a gift from Heaven.

We strolled across, Mr. Hare taking my elbow as we stepped over the uneven stone pavement, and paused at the crumbled parapet to admire the vast prospect over the fields and orchards. The portal to the old tower was secured by a thick wooden door, studded with nails and banded with iron but now fallen off its hinges. It merely leaned forlornly in its place, and a footman and gardener had to hoist it aside for us.

"Oh dear." Mr. Hare gazed open-mouthed up at the ruinous circular staircase that ascended in a majestic spiral inside the tower. Each tread was crumbled away in the center, and at the widest outer edge was merely an unstable slope of loose rock. A cascade of smaller gray stones clogged the stair, clearly fallen from above. To scale the stair, one had to shuffle this rubble aside to tread where each step was sturdiest. As one might expect, the least worn places were at the center of the spiral, where each tread was perhaps two inches wide. A thick rope had been affixed to ringbolts up the center of the stair, so at least there was a handhold. But a more intimidating ascent could hardly be imagined.

"Perhaps," Mr. Hare suggested, "this is too difficult an ascent for a lady of blood."

I had to laugh. "Oh, but now I see the stair, we must! Mr. Hare, have you ever heard of domestic tobogganing?"

"No indeed. What is it?"

"This is the ideal staircase for it! You find the

largest metal tea tray in the house, and sit on it to slide down the stair."

"Mrs. Camlet." Mr. Hare's eyes bulged. "A lady of your high breeding cannot have done this."

I, who have jiggered candles to improve a ghost story? It is a sad flaw in my character, but convenient fiction rises with distressing ease to my lips. It simply does not do, to tell men the truth. "Oh dear no, Mr. Hare," I said demurely. "Such pranks are only for the foolish."

"I am quite of your thinking, madam," Mr. Hare said with audible relief. "Perhaps I should be first to ascend, so that you may more easily see where to place your foot."

The stair ran clockwise, making a full turn for every level. Occasionally on that first spiral more of a tread was useable. As the stair became more ruinous I saw that Mr. Hare had as much notion of where to place his foot as he did of tatting lace. Matters were greatly complicated by the fact that the stair had a narrow slit window only at the outermost turn of its spiral, so that for much of the ascent we were in twilight. Mr. Hare slipped and skidded, at one point tumbling backwards and nearly falling onto me. Fortunately, I had a firm grip on the rope and was able to steady him.

"Test each step before putting your weight onto it," I advised from below. "Do not hesitate to push the scree to the outer edge and so clear a toehold. Forgive me, if I'm being too bossy, but you do not want to wrench your ankle."

Soothing male pride is a useful mask, allowing a lady to get her own way. Mr. Hare replied, "Not at all, Mrs. Camlet. Your kind thoughtfulness brings to mind my own dear mother, whose care for me was no less assiduous. She passed to her Heavenly reward only last year, and I still miss her sadly." He looked back to gaze soulfully down at me.

"Is that a door I see ahead?"

The portal on the first level had been barred with a timber too heavy for us to lift. This one on the second was entirely missing. The wooden floor of the chamber within was in such poor repair that we did not dare to step inside, but simply paused to rest on the threshold.

"Where can all of these stones have come from?" I wondered. "Not from the walls, which seem sound enough. Besides, the stones are small and gray, not golden."

Mr. Hare is knowledgeable about some things. "They're from the roof, dear lady. We use slate shingling in Britain, but here they use smaller stones— lauze, is the Occitan word. They're supported on chestnut-wood rafters and crosspieces, and if those should rot away…"

"A cascade of stones, as we see here. So this tower has no roof." I peered up and glimpsed the distant glow of daylight at the top. "How fortunate that the weather is dry."

"The stones are annoying now, but when milord comes to restore this tower he shall be glad of them. They can be gathered up, laid anew into place on fresh rafters, and thus a considerable savings achieved."

I took the lead for the final ascent. The final turn of the stair was indeed perilous. The loose lauze rocks slid at every touch, and behind me Mr. Hare moaned, "Take care, madam!"

At last we achieved the topmost floor. Here was the prison of La Dame Blanche. There was no sign of the blocks that had allegedly walled in her doorway. The portal was entirely doorless. Inside was a modest square chamber with a noble stone fireplace. The massive mantel shelf was almost as tall as I. The only furniture remaining was the worm-eaten wooden lid of a linen chest, obstructing the doorway. When I stepped over it I saw the plaster of the ceiling was long gone, and between the cobwebby rafters the slope of the lauze roof above was visible. "Somewhat more weatherproof than the roof over the turret stair," I remarked. "I doubt if that chimney still draws, however."

The window was broad and innocent of shutters, a portal for light and not defensive archery. It gave onto a glorious vista of lush fields, gold for the harvest. The river wound through them, bright as hammered metal. It was wonderfully romantic, and I leaned on the thick stone sill to hear the distant clank of bells and the tiny bleating of sheep from the other side of the steep valley. What a comfort this must have been to the imprisoned countess! "I've been imprisoned myself, in much less pleasant conditions—"

"Aaah!" A fearful cry! I whirled to see Mr. Hare pointing at the doorway. "Look!"

Against the shadow was a paleness. I bit back a scream. A chill seemed to flow from it. Mr. Hare cried, "It's the ghost of Simone, la Dame Blanche!"

He skittered backwards, caught his foot on the chest lid, and fell. His head made an audible thump as it struck the corner of the mantel. He toppled like a falling ninepin. Blood gushed copiously from the head wound, and formed a pool on the dusty flagstones.

"You silly man!" He didn't hear me. He had knocked himself quite senseless. I propped his head up on edge of the wooden lid and drew a handkerchief from my pocket to press firmly over the injury. "You shall need stitches—"

I gulped. The paleness was drawing nearer. It was indeed a spectre, the ghost of a woman! I could see the long skirts and massed hair. The chill was eerie. The cold of the stone floor struck right up through skirts and petticoats under my knees. I shrank back, shuddering.

But what with one thing and another, my instincts for peril are reliable. And now I had no sense of malice. If this was a woman, well then so am I. When I drew back the handkerchief slipped aside, and the blood trickled down the side of Mr. Hare's nose.

To my horror the supernatural visitant held out a ghostly finger, and dipped it into the scarlet flow. Was she a vampire? But then I remembered in the *Aeneid*. Virgil, and Dante after him, have assured us that ghosts require blood before they can speak.

"Are you Simone?" I demanded. "La Dame Blanche, imprisoned here by your husband?"

Her countenance was almost transparent, but I could discern large eyes, blinking short-sightedly in astonishment. "*M. le comte*, my husband? But no, Raymonde was of the nature most indulgent. When I wished to spend days at my pen, he made not the least complaint."

"You were free to leave this chamber?"

"Indeed, when I was not busy transcribing the chanson of Iseult." Her voice was thinning, becoming more distant. "There, you may see it." A smoke-pale finger pointed upwards. I stared and could just discern a dark mass in the corner where the biggest rafter was socketed into the stone. "Of your kindness, I implore you. Please show it to him."

"You mean..." I glanced down. Why would poor Mr. Hare want to see an ancient chanson? When I looked up again la Dame Blanche was so sheer as to be nearly invisible. As I watched she faded into nonentity again.

But my unfortunate companion was stirring, clapping a hand to his broken head. "Where is she?" he cried. "The ghost!"

"She spoke but a few words." I pressed the

handkerchief firmly to his wound again.

"And she's gone? Oh, no! No! Mr. Camlet looks for me to write about a supernatural visitation!"

"Your injury must be seen to," I said. "If I support you on the outer side I believe we may be able to descend."

I levered him upright, but his knees wobbled alarmingly. "Oh, I'm giddy," he groaned. "I cannot, I shall faint!"

Abruptly he slumped, catching his foot on the edge of the wooden chest lid. It slid as he collapsed on top of it with a thump. I fell to my knees and gripped the wooden rim as it teetered. "Mr. Hare, get up! You're going to fall down the stair!"

All the reply I got was a moan. The massive lid slipped alarmingly as the loose stones rattled down under its weight. Abruptly I realized that I had not the strength to haul it back up into the chamber. It was going to slide away, and Mr. Hare with it. "Mr. Hare! Mr. Hare!"

If the lid tore free of my fingers he would assuredly tumble out as it careened down the stair. Without thinking about it I flung myself forward, face down onto his supine form, just as my grip failed. I landed with my head between his boots, and we were off, careening helplessly down the stony spiral.

The loose stones rattled around us, cascading all around and bouncing on my back, thundering like a storm-lashed surf. Beneath me from somewhere near my feet Mr. Hare wailed in horror. "Stop, stop!" he shrieked. "What is happening? We shall be dashed to pieces!"

But domestic tobogganing with my children did supply some useful wisdom. I knew, from bandaging little Micah all those years ago, that it would be dangerous to hold onto the edges of the lid. As it smashed from side to side against the stone curve of the stair, my fingers would be crushed. Instead I braced my feet and elbows against the inside rim of the lid, wedging the both of us inside as we picked up downhill speed and caromed off the stone walls. If only we did not entirely overturn!

The descent took but moments, hardly time in my opinion to become terrified. The portal at the bottom of the stair still stood open. But since one is obliged to turn to step out into the courtyard, our halt was messy. The edge of the lid rammed the doorpost and I was flung off. I tumbled over and over like a rugger ball, and found myself lying at my astonished hostess's feet.

Mignonne shrieked something regrettable in her own tongue. Beside her Micah cried out in dismay. "Miss Marian, what are you at? Are you injured?"

"Dusty, but unhurt, thank you, dear." I allowed him to help me to my feet. My gown was grayish with stone dust, my cap was gone, and I had torn a hole in my sleeve.

"What a hooligan you are, Marian," Mignonne exclaimed. "You have not altered a hair since you were seventeen!"

And Mr. Hare astonished me by bounding to his feet. "How could you do this to me," he wailed. "I am injured, I'm ill! My nerves shall never recover!"

"You assured me, Mr. Hare, that you could neither rise nor walk," I snapped. "If I had known you were so spry, I would have put less effort into your rescue."

He did not even have the grace to blush. "My lady, we saw the ghost! La Dame Blanche! Mr. Camlet, it was shocking! See how I am injured!"

"He fell onto the edge of the mantel," I explained. "And, Mignonne, Lady Simone did not profess herself to be cruelly imprisoned. She deliberately sequestered herself, and pointed out to me her project. It's hidden up in the rafters."

"A treasure!" Mignonne cried. "How pleased Henri will be! Quick, quick, Marian. You must show me!"

Mr. Hare slumped against the wall, moaning with melodramatic pathos.

"He may need stitches," I had to concede.

A hospitable hostess, the marquise immediately commanded, "Alphonse, have him helped to bed. Let Gavroche ride to the village, and fetch the doctor to attend him. And, for us, a ladder and ropes, immediately!"

Micah is very strong, and Mignonne's footmen assisted us so that climbing the ruinous stair was far simpler this time. The long ladder was more easily hoisted from the uppermost window with a rope and pulley, and I arranged for the much-abused wooden chest lid to be drawn up as well, so that all of Mignonne's furnishings would be restored to their proper place.

"And your sliding, Marian!" The marquise, wedged securely inside the stone spiral on either side by sturdy manservants, was free to eloquently wave her hands. "Such a thing never would have occurred to me. And this stair is ideal for it! Where did you learn such pranks?"

"I am pleased to say it was my stepson here who taught me the way of it," I declared with truth.

"M. Camlet? Indeed!" Mignonne actually turned to peer past me at him.

"It's a common naughtiness among English schoolboys, my lady." There was definitely a note of alarm in Micah's voice. "Somewhat rowdy, but nothing unusual."

We paused at the second level to rest. Micah went on, and I took the opportunity to say, "Although Lady

Simone does not seem to have been actually imprisoned—"

"Oh Marian, Henri shall not like that. A chateau must have an unhappy ghost, it is *de rigueur*."

"Nevertheless," I persisted, "it is true, then and now, that a husband has complete dominion over his wife in these matters. Even today, a man may slay an adulterous wife outright, with impunity."

"Is that indeed so?"

Carefully I avoided meeting her startled glance. "Certainly. In England and in France, the passion of the moment is a solid defense in court for a husband even today. And the fourteenth century was a far more rough-and-ready time. That Lady Simone survived suggests that adultery was not an issue in her case."

When we achieved the third story the haunted chamber was just as I had left it. There was no sign of any pale spectre or supernatural chill. Micah was supervising the men hauling the ladder up from below. As soon as it arrived he said, "And where is this treasure, Miss Marian?"

"She said nothing of what it is," I warned. "She only pointed, there, and said that I should show it to him."

Micah leaned the ladder on the rafter indicated and a footman steadied it as he climbed handily up. Mignonne said, "Who is this 'him' of which she speaks?"

"She didn't say. Perhaps Mr. Hare?"

"He was unconscious, you said."

Or shamming! "Certainly he was the only male present," I noted.

But Micah had achieved the rafter now. "There's an old wooden box up here all right, shoved back against the wall. I expect that as long as the plaster ceiling was sound no one could see it. But I can't shift it. We need a crowbar."

The footmen at the rope called the order down to their fellows below. A pry bar had to be fetched from the carriage house, but the interval was usefully employed with hauling the battered chest lid back up. With a tool in hand Micah was able to loosen the box from where it had frozen in place by the passing decades. "It's falling apart," he said. "Is there a sack or anything?"

"My shawl," Mignonne suggested. "But no, it is cashmere. Luc, do you lend Mr. Camlet your coat."

This was done, and the cracked and crumbling relic was lowered down, Micah scrambling after. "It's not metal inside," he reported. "Not heavy enough."

"The ghost said it was a chanson, the chanson de Iseult," I recalled. "Not one that I've ever heard of."

"But, how disappointing." Mignonne peered into the bundle. "Cloth?"

"No, it's parchment," Micah said, lifting a yellowed scrap. "Leather, treated to be written upon." Suddenly he turned quite pale. "Miss Marian, what if it's for me? Oh Lord, could it be…a *submission*?"

I began to laugh. "My poor son! If even the ghosts of authors yearn for publication, the number of hopeful contributors to *Gadsbee's* is truly infinite!"

But Micah has already learned well the essential business skill of passing the baby along. "My lady, this must be for his lordship to decide," he immediately said to Mignonne. "As the heir and descendant of the authoress, the marquis should consider having the entire artifact evaluated by men of learning, perhaps at the University of Bordeaux. They'll be able to read the antique Occitan dialect and evaluate the manuscript's genuineness and literary merit."

"Let it be so," the marquise said. "Luc, do you carry the chest carefully down, and set it in milord's library. Not on his table, the box is so dirty. Perhaps on the carpet by his chair. I fear, dear Marian, that Henri will far prefer la Dame Blanche to continue as the story of an imprisoned lady of the amorous spirit. A busy authoress, how shall that be even a quarter as romantic? One has a duty to the chateau's reputation! But I shall tell my husband all, and he shall decide."

"As is his duty," I conceded. Perhaps if the marquis came up to this chamber himself Lady Simone could persuade him.

"But now!" Her ladyship beamed upon us, her great dark eyes sparkling. "I have a fresh notion of the most magnificent. You, M. Camlet, shall introduce me to the art of sliding down stairs!"

Again my stepson was deft. "Miss Marian, you must come too. I know you enjoy domestic tobogganing as well as any lad. Show us the gentle ladies' way of it, if you would."

What could I say? "Well, it is dreadfully thrilling, and both our hostess and I adore excitement, is it not so, Mignonne? Dear, you must turn the chest lid over for us. I expect there shall be just room for three to sit. Mignonne, you're the littlest, and must be in front."

Squeaking with excitement, the marquise allowed herself to be handed in. I tucked her long full skirts well in around her legs. "Do you know, my dear Marian," she said in French, "perhaps you are right. Adventures are safer if they involve sledding down slopes."

"I think you'll find this thrilling enough," I said. "Be sure to keep your fingers inside."

"And Miss Marian next," Micah said. "That's the way, like peas in a pod. As the heaviest I should be at the back. Are we all ready? Then let us be off. Luc, if you would give us a push!"

Brenda W. Clough is the first female Asian-American SF writer, first appearing in print in 1984. Her novella 'May Be Some Time' was a finalist for both the Hugo and the Nebula awards and became the novel *Revise the World*. Her latest time travel trilogy is *Edge to Center*, available at Book View Café. *Marian Halcombe*, a series of eleven neo-Victorian thrillers appeared in 2021. Her complete bibliography is up on her web page, www.brendaclough.net.

About the story

When I was in France I visited the Chateau de Puymartin (https://www.chateau-puymartin.com/) A perfect fairy-tale chateau, it is perched on a height overlooking an idyllic countryside, complete with gardens and towers, ruinous and haunted. The ghost, however, was annoying. Adulterous wife walled up by M. le count, bah. Cliched. What is this, the 14th century? Well, it was. But set the story in 1870 and Marian Halcombe Camlet can fix it.

Given to the Sunrise

Dave Smeds

Leander Gorham had never been afraid of ghosts. They were snowfall in the night. You could stand there and let the flakes kiss your cheeks, or you could go inside and sit by the hearth, untouched.

That was before the Sickly Season fever came up the Wabash to ravage Vincennes, claiming Leander's two young children and then his wife over the span of only three days. After they were consigned to their rest in the city graveyard, he moved out of the cottage behind the wagonwright's shop, no matter the laughter and love he had known within those walls. He abandoned Vincennes altogether, fleeing into Illinois Territory. He did not stop and build his log cabin until he had satisfied himself that he would have no neighbor near enough to notice his chimney smoke or hear his dog bark.

For six months, his solitude was undisturbed. Then one icy morning as he was chopping kindling at the stump, his bulldog rose up on his stubby legs, hackles high, and whined.

The hatchet tumbled out of Leander's grip. His heart began to pound.

"Almeda? Is that you?" he called.

Bo was gazing intently at a gap in the trees to the west. Leander studied the spot. He saw nothing more than the saplings he had recently cut down. He was planning to split them to make fence rails.

The chickens retreated into their coop. Bo acted like he wanted to follow them.

This could only be what he had feared, but as far as Leander could see, there was no avoiding it. If all the running he had done had not saved him, the only protection he could ever have would arise out of mercy.

He took a deep breath and marched forward.

He stopped when he reached the stack of trimmed saplings. He still saw nothing that didn't belong. But that was the way of it. A haunting did not begin by occupation. It began by removal. Whatever ought to be there—a cloud of gnats, the aroma of leaf litter and moss—was absent. A space had been made in the world. Gradually the ghost would learn how to inhabit it.

"Darling. I can't bear it," Leander whispered. "You have to let me be."

He was answered only by silence, but that in itself was an answer. The woods had a thousand voices, of bees, of squirrels, of woodpeckers, but all of them had paused.

"This isn't your place," he added. "You know that."

And again, only silence.

He was about to leave when he happened to look straight down. There in the leaf litter and mushrooms were two objects he had not noticed when he had been cutting down the saplings: a stone mortar and its pestle.

His fear dissipated. A visitation this might be, but not of the shade of his wife, nor of his precious little Rosemary or Elias.

He returned to his cabin, went to the hogshead where he stored his kitchen corn, and scooped a few kernels into his palm. He took this small measure back to the clearing, placed it in the bowl of the mortar, and in the fashion of a Shawnee woman he had once observed, ground it into meal.

He left the artifacts in place and retreated ten paces.

The sense of inhabitation remained, but the restlessness was tempered. Birds were twittering in the trees again.

"I don't mean any harm," Leander said. "I hope you don't, either."

Leander hoped his gesture might bring the matter to an end. It did not. Two days later he was churning butter and the hair on the back of his neck stood up, just as if a spider were crawling out of his collar—but there was no spider, only the reaction by his own body. The next day, Bo suddenly got up and hid in the corner behind the water barrel. Later in the week, the milk cow began making a fuss an hour before dawn, costing Leander the last fragment of his night's sleep, the portion he treasured most.

Plain goodwill on his part was not enough, it seemed. The ghost needed something further.

Leander considered the matter, and over the course of that day, in addition to his regular chores, he carried several large stones to a patch of bare earth some fifteen paces from where the mortar and pestle lay. With them, he created a firepit. When evening came and he had eaten his supper, he dressed warmly, brought out his sturdiest chair—the one his grandfather had made—and began to wait.

Nothing came of it at first. After a few hours, he returned to his cabin and went to bed, finding only the ash of the watchfire in the morning. Another night brought the same result.

On the third evening, his toes grew so cold he considered ending his session early. But he tossed another piece of cordwood on the blaze. Finally his patience was rewarded. A misty silhouette formed in the clearing. Gradually it took on more substance and even an impression of color.

Leander had expected to see wrinkles, a bent spine, a halo of wispy grey. Instead he was greeted by unlined brown skin, supple posture, and a long braid of glossy black hair. She had been claimed by death when she was barely a woman at all. The only maturity was in her pose, solemn and mournful, eyes downcast.

She was unclothed except for her burial shroud. The thin blanket was simple and unadorned and gave him no insight as to what band of native people she had belonged to. And who was to say how long ago she had died, and where? Perhaps the mortar and pestle had been carried about for generations and great distances before being abandoned. She might have been part of a tribe that no longer existed.

The chances that she had ever in life used the English language were poor. Nevertheless, he asked his question. "What is it you want?"

As soon as he uttered the words, she lifted her head and fixed her gaze upon him for the few moments she could manage to remain substantial enough to be seen.

Leander and the ghost observed an accord from that point on, or at least that's how he characterized their dealings. He installed a post and brace from which to hang a lantern and nearly every evening, put in a stint by the fire, sometimes sitting, sometimes pacing. On those occasions when he was too busy to linger, he still made sure to step outside his cabin and face the haunted glade, demonstrating to her that she could depend on his attention. In return, she stopped pestering him or his critters.

Her appearances were brief, sometimes extremely so. Throughout every visitation, she would stare at him. Leander never had the impression she was angry with him. No, it was a plea of some kind. He was sure of that, even though she never once wept or fell on her knees or attempted any sort of sign language.

Leander knew there must be something specific he could do for her, but he couldn't puzzle it out. All he could do was maintain the ritual and hope his faithfulness alone provided some measure of comfort.

The weeks went on. Spring arrived. Leander finished fencing off five acres of prairie south of the cabin.

A proper homesteader would put more land into production in the first year of occupation, but Leander did not see the point. He had no family to support. He just needed to raise enough wheat, potatoes, corn, and hay to tide him and Bo and the cow and the chickens over the winter to come.

He went to the trading post and rented a breaking plow and nine yoke of oxen—a significant expense, but he had long since set aside the funds. He couldn't do much planting if he left the parcel in its primordial state.

The team cooperated as well as any oxen he had ever worked. All Leander had to do to get them moving was to talk to them in an encouraging way and flick the lash in the air in the general vicinity of their hindquarters. He began by plowing the far edge of the field and worked back toward the cabin. In his wake, over-turned topsoil and the uprooted remains of native grasses and shrubs exuded a fine, fecund aroma. He began to feel less like a frontiersman and more like a farmer, a role more in keeping with his nature.

Less than halfway through the third day he was on the verge of completing the job. The edge of the tilled ground had come to within a stone's throw of the fence he had erected along the edge of the timber.

Suddenly the team stopped.

That was that. No matter how sweet his tone or how many times Leander snapped the whip, they would not push onward.

He refused to apply the leather to their flesh. He didn't believe in that. Besides, there could be only one explanation for their change in attitude. The ghost was meddling.

Leander weighed his progress. Four and a half acres was nearly the same thing as five. And if he quit now, he could get the team back to the trading post by evening, a day ahead of schedule, and ask the owner for a partial refund. So he did precisely that.

He arrived back home at sunset. He went at once to the glade.

Apparently the ghost had felt encroached upon by the plowing. That perplexed him. Her bower lay on the other side of the fence, outside the intended bounds of his plot. It would not have been destroyed. Hadn't that been obvious?

Bo joined him. The dog still would not approach the haunting on his own, but he would do so if Leander was there. Together they waited.

Sunset deepened into gloaming. The shadows beneath the branches became a backdrop dark enough that when the ghost materialized, she was as easy to see as she was at night.

"Huh!" blurted Leander.

She did not maintain the usual stare. Once she confirmed that he was watching, she knelt, facing the earth, and moved her hand as if she had a stick in it and was poking downward with it. She then tilted her empty palm and made a smoothing-over motion at the level of her feet.

As ever, she was not able to stay long. She vanished before Leander grasped what he had witnessed, but belatedly it came to him. She had been miming the process of making holes in loose ground and planting seeds.

Leander decided that could mean only one thing. And certainly it wouldn't hurt him if the assumption turned out in the long run to be incorrect.

Most of the farm planted his way. Half an acre rendered her way. He would see to it.

The ghost did not become fully visible again for many weeks. He was not surprised by that, not after the way she had exerted herself.

In those weeks, he labored from daybreak to nightfall, sowing and planting. Early on, he visited the trading post, not only to obtain a suitable variety of seeds, but to consult with a middle-aged trapper who had spent several years growing up as an adoptee among a band of Fox, or Meskwaki as the trapper sometimes referred to them. The man refreshed Leander's understanding of how to raise crops the way they had been grown in these tallgrass prairie lands before the era of the white man: not in rows with furrows, but in a chaotic fellowship of species. His advisor even sketched out a rendering of three tall stalks of maize jutting skyward out of a tangle of squash, beans, and tomato vines.

Leander followed the advice as best he could. He raked the thickest clumps of last year's growth into even bigger piles and torched them. He didn't happen to have any bison to clomp around, but he put his cow out to graze for a few days, after which he got out his shovel and hoe and loosened up a spot of dirt here, a spot there, distributing the ash and dung as he went. After a pleasant two days down at the creek, he had a gratifying number of fish to bury beside and among the seeds.

Corn, yes. Three types of squash including pumpkin. Two types of beans. Those made up the main tangles, with the tomatoes less intermingled. Here and there, between each of the main clumps, he added chili peppers.

And over at the edge of the plot, in the vicinity of the cabin, he planted watermelon. He didn't think the ghost would mind, and it was where he had intended all along to put his garden.

No late frost ruined his progress. Rainfall came at useful intervals, and not too much on any single occasion. Green growth thrust out of the soil.

Eventually the ghost began manifesting again. Mornings seemed to be easiest for her. Leander would come out of his cabin and en route to the milking shed would find her in place, ornamenting the dawn. Sometimes she would not vanish until the first direct rays of sunshine made her impossible to see, and even then, she wasn't always entirely dismissed. He could tell from the way butterflies dodged aside or crickets refused to chirp.

She still stared at him, but not in the intense way she had before. Leander grew accustomed to the observation. On those rare occasions when he found himself craving privacy, he would move off where she had no vantage of him, shackled as she was to the glade.

The warmest weeks of summer arrived. The mosquitoes enjoyed this far too much. Leander swore at them as he slapped dead those that came within reach, but the truth was, he was relieved by how comparatively few there were. He was accustomed to the bloodsucking hordes that clouded the banks of the Wabash, the offspring of the stagnant pools left after the earthquakes had disrupted the old course of the river.

Once the first of the crops ripened, Leander became greatly occupied. Naturally much of his attention was directed toward harvesting his main fields, but he did not neglect the ghost's half acre. He even thought to place an ear of multi-colored maize near the mortar, added a small pumpkin and a gourd.

By that point, he had the confirmation of his hunch. The more the land around her came to resemble the sort of surroundings she had inhabited while she was an incarnate being, the stronger her presence.

And what would she do when she was strong enough to do it? One morning in late September, he had his answer. The ghost turned and walked away, heading deeper into the woods—*away from her anchor.*

After two steps, she checked to see that Leander was watching. Three steps more and she faded away.

All that strength, built up over half a year, and that was what had come of it. Five steps.

Leander called Bo to him. Even if no scent trail existed to follow, the bulldog was his regular companion when he hunted, and he wanted the luck that came from joint effort. Together they set out. At first Leander tried to step on the very spots the ghost had, as best he could determine. Eventually he was forced to guess what her route would have been.

The stretch of timber was already known to him. He had ventured this way any number of times while collecting firewood, or cutting more saplings for fence rails, or hunting game. More than once he had deliberately searched for traces of anything that might be connected to the ghost, but he had never done so as intently as he did now.

He saw deer beds, coon scat, rodent bones beneath an owl hollow. Anything else was of that sort—things that belonged. Two miles from the cabin he came to the other side where the landscape opened up again. There he gave up, because any potential discovery would only be hidden in the tallgrass, or trampled by the occasional wagon that had passed through on the way to the brine fields.

He trudged back, examining everything he could think of, even the upper canopy of the beeches and oaks. Bo startled a mother quail from its nest in a gooseberry bramble, a fine thing if they had been searching for quail eggs, but of no consequence on this day.

The closer he came to the starting point, the slower he went, and the more he shook his head. When he came to the glade, he stood right beside the mortar and pestle and the little shrine of produce he had created.

He sighed. "It was no good. I don't know what you meant to tell me. I'm sorry."

And of course there was no reply.

Leander had always regarded deep autumn as his favorite time of the year, when the region's mugginess went into exile and the forest floor became a collage of nature. Best of all, the crop acreage did not need tending as it did in the warm months; he could allow himself a day off, or even three. He had thought he would welcome the season's arrival. Yet each morning when he rose and saw no sign of his spectral neighbor, he considered going back to bed.

The hole in the world was still there within the glade. He could still sense it. But the ghost did not dominate it as she once had. She did not quicken to visibility. Rodents that had earlier avoided the bower moved in and nibbled a hole into the pumpkin and the next day ants were all over it.

He had helped her grow strong. Now that coin was spent.

What could he do now? More of the same? All the way to another harvest season? Would the haunting even last as long as that?

No. He had failed her. All that was left now, he supposed, was the vigil.

A vigil was a thing he knew how to do. He'd first learned how at the age of nine when his great-grandmother Olivia was approaching her last breath. The white-haired matriarch slipped into what everyone recognized was her final decline. It was the very busiest time of the year. Leander's father could not afford time away from the fields. His mother was occupied with the cooking and household responsibilities and the infant on her hip. It therefore fell to Leander and his little brother Caleb and their crippled uncle Silas to sit with the dying old lady. It did not matter that Olivia barely seemed to be aware of their presence. "No one should die alone," declared Leander's father.

The process had taken three weeks. Expecting two young boys to sit there and maintain decorum day after day? It was a tall order. But as a peg-leg veteran, their uncle had been part of more than one vigil. He knew a trick.

He read books.

It was more than that, though. Silas had seemed to understand what a twitchy pair of youngsters would appreciate, exposing Leander and Caleb to the adventures of Robinson Crusoe or selections from Shakespeare, skipping entirely the dreary works their schoolmarm imagined would instill a proper Puritan ethic within them. The hours passed without arguments and only a modest amount of fidgeting, and when Olivia finally succumbed, Leander had no anger toward her for the inconvenience she had put him through.

Unfortunately Leander's cabin was completely bereft of books, unless he counted his almanac. He was even lacking a Holy Bible, the household copy having been placed in the coffin with Almeda because she had derived so much comfort from its pages. What he did have, though, was the knack of carrying on a conversation all by himself. All he needed was to fix his attention on a subject, be it a memory, or a way of looking at the world, or the retelling of something once told to him, and he could go on and on about it. He did not need anyone else to ask a question or throw in a contribution. Somehow the sentences would come, one after the other.

And so he accepted the obligation. He moved a large supply of wood near the firepit he had created at the beginning of his acquaintance with the ghost, and kept a blaze going within the circle of stones at all times. He also erected a tripod of stout branches and suspended a cauldron.

When all this was ready, he cooked.

"Have you ever had porridge?" he asked as he poured in a measure of oats. "My father's mother was a Highlander. You couldn't get her to begin a day without a serving."

He went on, describing his grandmother, and his great-grandmother, and Uncle Silas, and anyone else he had known whose nature or whose life had a twist that shaped them in a way a listener might find worth hearing about. That alone filled up many hours, in part because he spoke of his own life. It didn't seem right to leave that out. He hoped he was not being vain. He did not exaggerate his accomplishments. Mainly he spoke of what his hopes had been, setting out as a young man.

The fables of Aesop served him in good stead, because he remembered so many and found it easy to embellish them until they filled the allotted length of time. "My favorite is the one about the fox and the grapes," he told her. And indeed it was. He liked the way the story had only one character. No antagonist. No ally. No one to utter the moral. Just a creature left to its own nature and its own devices to make its judgment about the world. And who was to say the fox was wrong? The grapes probably *were* sour.

He sat during the afternoons, sometimes for long stretches. He put in sessions in the evening. And most of all, he made sure to come out at dawn, padding the chair with a blanket he had warmed inside the cabin, building up the campfire and rubbing his gloved hands over it, and having bites of his breakfast—porridge or otherwise—during the pauses in his narrations.

At times, his devotion to the effort weakened, particularly when truly frigid air rolled over the land from the northwest or from the lakes. More than once, he had no choice but to hole up in his cabin. Emerging from the longest of those retreats, his fears were realized as he detected no remnant of the haunting.

He was embarrassed by the relief that flooded into him. The ending was not satisfactory, but at least it *was* an ending, and he could say he had done his best.

But as he completed the short walk and stood beside the lantern post, he realized his impression might be wrong. The ghost might be there after all, her presence now so subtle it was like Bo's heartbeat against his calf as the dog leaned into him, questing for a share of body heat.

He dug down in the lee of the tripod, uncovered the bed of ash and charcoal, and lit a fresh fire. Even with that, it was too cold to be seated. Too cold to breathe, really. But he began reciting tales of the hardest winters he had known, of the length of the icicles from the eaves of the family barn, of the thickness of the pelt on the muskrat his brother Caleb snared. He managed to remain in place long enough to become certain he was not simply casting words into the air, but still in fact had a listener.

Again and again he came. Slowly the haunting regained some morsel of its former potency, some hint of intention.

In February came a warm spell, or that is to say, a warm spell by the standard of the season, reducing the snow banks to an ankle-high blanket of whiteness over the landscape. The atmosphere was no longer crystalline but gossamer.

The night was well gone, but all at once an owl floated past, heading into the trees, a bright-eyed not-yet-bloodied mouse wrapped in its talons.

"Will you look at that?"

Bo was beside him as always, but Leander had not meant the comment for the dog. He said it as if he was in the company of a human companion, as if he might get a reply.

As his glance dropped from the treetops where the owl had vanished and settled on the haunted glade, the woman's shape manifested. The lack of glare rendered her distinct enough that Leander could see she was not arranged in the usual way. Her head was tilted downward. Her arms were folded across her midsection.

As a man who had once been a father, he knew that pose. The ghost couldn't make the baby visible any more than she had been able to make the stick visible or clothe herself in anything more than her burial shroud, but she could show herself as she had been when she had held an infant. A newborn. He was sure from the small, nestlike configuration of the embrace, from the cupping of one palm so that the infant's head would not flop back.

"Oh, Lord!" exclaimed Leander.

As young as she had seemed to be, he had never thought of her as a mother.

The ghost evaporated from sight, but she had done enough. Leander understood. He slipped through the fence and faced the woods, preparing to set out again in the direction she had indicated at the end of summer.

This time, he took a moment before rushing off. He knelt down and dug through the snow until he found the pestle. Removing the glove from his left hand, he reached out.

By rights, the stone should have been so cold against his skin as to be painful. But his palm was untroubled, as if he had been holding the object for several minutes and it had absorbed some of his own heat.

He walked forward one careful step at a time, taking in the surroundings with as much attentiveness as he could muster, not allowing Bo to forge ahead. The marks in the snow to his right—those had been made by a stoat. The broken branch over his head—that was new damage, no doubt a consequence of the storm a fortnight past.

By the time he was halfway through the stand of timber, the pestle lost its extra heat. He pressed it more firmly into his palm. The change was so subtle he could easily have convinced himself it was an illusion, but he needed the guidance and chose to have faith in it. He reversed course. Within a few steps, the warmth was rekindled.

The phenomenon was strongest when he was in

the midst of a circle of saplings all about the same age, trees that occupied what must have been, a decade or two in the past, a small clearing. He studied the spot, and finally he saw what had been impossible to discern in late summer due to the leafiness of the overhanging branches: a mound. It was about three feet long and two feet wide. At its head stood a broken stick placed upright in the ground like a post. A horizontal stick was attached to form a cross. On Leander's prior exploration, the artifact had apparently been obscured behind a frond of bracken.

The twine and pitch that had been used to bind the pieces of wood had become blackened and frayed. The marker would have fallen apart and been unrecognizable in another year or two or three. Leander no longer had to wonder that the ghost might belong to a woman who had died in ancient times. She had been alive recently enough that when her child's body had been placed here in this ground, it had been done in a Christian fashion.

Whoever had undertaken the burial had surely meant well. But what they had done was not proper. Otherwise there would not be a ghost mother haunting his farm.

Leander believed he could do better. Perhaps it would be better enough.

First, he needed tools and materials. He returned to his homestead and gathered up his ax, his shovel, and a doeskin he had been drying and stretching on a rack. These he brought to the gravesite.

With the ax, he loosened bark from the trunks of nearby fallen trees until he had collected a generous stack of various sizes and shapes. He made curved poles from the thin branches of a dormant buckeye and piled them within easy reach.

Now for the grave itself. The orientation was

wrong—lengthwise from north to south. It needed to be west to east. He decided he would not try to adjust the existing trench, but would make a new one. He moved several paces from the existing mound and begin digging.

The loam layer on top gave way easily. The compacted soil below, threaded with roots, required considerably more effort. More than once, he paused to wipe sweat from his face.

Four feet deep was right, if his memory served. Not six. After he had lifted out a pair of large rocks, he achieved that depth within the hour. After smoothing out the bottom, he lined it with a layer of bark.

The truly unwelcome part of the process was the disinterment. The mound was however made of dirt that had already been worked, and after he went along the edges to loosen the material, he did not have to struggle to get through it. The opposite was true. He had to move deliberately, removing only a small amount with each dip of the shovel. Eventually he was barely using the tool at all. Cold as the ground was, he proceeded by hand whenever possible.

Gradually he was able to confirm the contours of the grave's occupant. The remains were wrapped in a decomposing shawl. It was made of wool woven in the European way. He peeled it aside.

What he discovered were not the remains of a newborn. The front of the skull was fully fused above the brow, and the jaws contained a few teeth. The mother might well have died within days of giving birth, but her offspring had survived a good portion of its first year. When the infant finally had died, the absence of a living mother might have been one of the reasons the burial had not happened according to native practices.

With reverence, Leander wrapped the little one

within the deerskin and placed the bundle atop the bark bed in the new grave. He wove a lattice of buckeye poles over it as a shelter, and laid more bark atop the structure to form a roof. Then he gently tossed on shovel-loads of dirt until the hole was full, and then he added more to create a mound.

The last stage took up most of the remainder of the day: He laid branches down and tied them and placed more slabs of bark around until the mound was encapsulated in a tiny grave house. He left one small opening.

The grave was arranged so that when the sun rose in the morning, the child would be positioned to greet it.

He surveyed his handiwork. What he had done reasonably matched the Shawnee graves he had seen. He knew certain other tribes of the region laid their dead to rest in much the same way. Would this be sufficient? Or was the funeral ritual also required? As far as Leander was aware, that required family members. What hope did he have of identifying such kinfolk, much less tracking them down? Even enlisting the assistance of a random group of Shawnee struck him as next to impossible. None were likely to be approachable given the nasty business of the past few years with Tecumseh and his brother the Prophet, and the blood spilled.

For now, he had done as much as he could do. He slapped the dirt from his gloves, gathered his shovel and ax, and marched back to his cabin.

Weary as he was, he had trouble sleeping that night, restless with anticipation. He rose even earlier than he had planned to, well before the cow needed her milking. It was still full dark when he set out from the homestead, wrapped in his heaviest cloak and fortified with a serving of hot venison stew. By the time he reached the gravesite, the first purple tones of crepuscular light were only just beginning to lay claim to the eastern horizon.

His first hint that all might be well was the way the forest and its denizens awoke around him. The hush of night was replaced by the natural music of bird twitter and dripping branches. A sweetness of hulled bark rose from the mound. These were not the sounds and aromas of imprisonment, but of release.

Sunlight brightened the treetops and gradually made its way down the trunks. Finally a ray touched the little grave house.

A veil of whiteness fluttered out of the little door and whisked away upward. It happened so quickly Leander would have missed it if he had blinked. Beside him, Bo stared at the branches as if wondering where it had gone. He gave one quick, cheerful, bulldog *whuff.*

Leander found himself needing to wipe his eyes.

One thing left to determine. Leander could barely breathe as he journeyed back to the glade near his cabin.

She was gone. It wasn't that her presence was faint or had been reduced to indirect signs. She was simply not there at all. The haunting had been for a purpose, and the purpose was fulfilled. She had moved on.

Removing the pestle from the pouch at his belt, Leander restored it to the concave pit of the mortar.

He patted his dog on the back. "Looks like it's just you and me now, Bo."

❖

During the vestige of winter that remained, Leander cleared some timber, split more rails, and built fences. In the spring, he rented the breaking team again and got another five acres into cultivation. A man came up from Tennessee with his family and settled half a mile to the south by the grand white oak—conveniently out of sight, but close enough that Leander could hire the twelve-year-old son to help him get his planting done on schedule.

As his acquaintance with his new neighbors solidified, he took to seeking out their company, even becoming a regular in their home for Sunday dinner. Soon he was finding his way to the trading post every Tuesday morning for coffee with the locals there.

He did not go so far as to invite others to visit his own cabin, but the absence of a spinning wheel in the corner or an apron outside on the laundry line began to gnaw at his peace of mind. Now that the memory of Almeda and the children no longer burned as sharply, he began to concede to himself, in the quiet moments and never once in his letters to his relatives back east, that he was not naturally suited to a solitary existence.

But to do something about it? Not yet. Not yet.

He depended upon the land and his chores for distraction. Certainly there was always plenty to do. His traditionally-planted fields grew more abundant and more tidy all the time. He kept up the plot he had made for the ghost, though he was more experimental with the squash, there being so very many types to choose from. He also expanded the melon patch, not only in size but variety, supplementing the watermelon with musk melon.

He would still, of a morning, build a fire outdoors in the firepit and set a kettle of beans to simmer through the day, and of an evening, might bring out a bowl, take up residence in the glow of his hanging lantern, and eat. He was doing that very thing, contemplating the cresc-ent moon hanging in the purple and orange bands of the western sky, when Bo suddenly sat up.

Leander turned. There was the ghost in her usual spot.

Her shroud was wrapped around her more artfully

than before. Her hair glistened as though she had combed it thoroughly out and taken her time restoring a perfect braid.

She was smiling.

"Took you long enough," Leander quipped. "Though that did give me time to send for something I ought to have never been without."

He reached into the satchel he'd hung on the back of the chair, and removed the book it contained. "This was one of my uncle's favorites."

He set the volume on his lap and opened it to page one.

Dave Smeds is the author of novels, screenplays, comic book scripts, non-fiction articles, and more. His output extends across a range of genres including science fiction, sword-and-sorcery, superhero, alternate history, horror, erotica, contemporary fantasy, and young-adult. A major career focus is short fiction. His stories have appeared in such venues as the magazines *Asimov's Science Fiction*, *F&SF*, *Realms of Fantasy*, and *Dark Regions*, and anthologies such as *Full Spectrum 4*, *Peter S. Beagle's Immortal Unicorn*, *In the Field of Fire*, *The Shimmering Door*, *Return to Avalon*, *Lace and Blade*, and many volumes of the Sword and Sorceress series. He lives in Santa Rosa, CA with his wife and son.

About the story

Some of my ancestors were pioneers of the Ohio Valley. That includes my great great great grandmother Rachel Starr. Her nephew Esau Johnson—born in the year 1800, making him only one year younger than

Rachel—wrote a book-length memoir of his life, including extensive passages about his boyhood and youth, which he spent on the very edge of the frontier in first Ohio and then in Illinois. It is stunningly rich with context. Esau wasn't a historian writing about the major political and military events of an era and place he knew only from research. Instead, he described what life was actually like for the real folk who inhabited that part of the world at that point in time. The portrait captured in this never-published manuscript is profoundly different than what one might read in so-called "pioneer" fiction. The latter inevitably addresses other regions and/or other eras when such things as steamboats, railroads, bridges, and widespread literacy had transformed the settler way of life. I have itched for the chance to present a glimpse of what I regard as under-appreciated and far-too-little-understood early days. To get to do so in the form of a ghost story was a bonus.

Lideric

Jennifer Stevenson

"Mom, Mom, I think this house is haunted after all!"

"That's nice, honey."

"The man said it wasn't haunted but it is!"

"Are you sure?"

"Mom, can I have some bread dough?"

"I gave you some."

"I put it in the barn for the rats. You said this farm has been deserted so long, even the rats are starving. I didn't see any."

"You have to wait to see a rat. They won't come out if they think you're watching."

"Like ghosts, right, Mom?"

"Why don't you go watch for the rats? You may have to wait a long time."

"I waited a long time already! Can I have more bread dough? It's for the ghost."

"The bread's in the oven, honey."

"Can you make some more?"

"I'm getting ready to paint this room. Maybe later."

"Can I go in the storm cellar and talk to the ghost?"

"Yes."

"I'll ask him if he likes bread dough."

"You do that."

"Because if the rats don't want it I can bring it down to the cellar."

"Exactly."

"Everybody says ghosts are hungry."

"I bet they are."

"But I don't want to take food away from the rats if he doesn't like it. Do you think he likes it? You don't like bread dough but I do."

"I would ask him, honey."

"I love bread dough!"

"I know you do."

"But I'll ask first, because I would eat it if he doesn't."

"Go ask him now, honey."

"He might not answer. He doesn't talk yet."

"I'm sure you'll find a way to make him answer."

"Or I could paint. I'm a good painter."

"Honey?"

"Can I help you paint?"

"Go play in the storm cellar!"

❖

"Hey mister."

"Ugh."

"Hey mister, are you dead or are you asleep?"

"Go away."

"Hey mister, where'd you come from?"

"I live here."

"Hey mister, let's play bears."

"Ugh."

"I could bring you bread dough, if the rats didn't get it."

"What year is it?"

"I'm five."

"That's not what I asked."

"I was four, but then I became five."

"Shut the door, kid, I'm trying to sleep."

"Dead people don't sleep. They only em-you-late real life."

"I'm not dead."

"If you were dead, you would be a ghost."

"Grrrr."

"How long did you sleep so far?"

"I don't know. What year is it?"

"I don't know. This farm was listed for twelve years. The man said."

"Ugh. Twelve years. I can't believe they were able to sell it."

"We're renting. Did you sleep for twelve years?"

"Apparently."

"Are you going to keep sleeping?"

"I don't know. How long are you going to live here?"

"We don't live anywhere very long."

"So there's hope."

"Mom had a boyfriend but he went away. And then we went away."

"And she's heartbroken, right?"

"She's painting her bedroom. She cried a lot when Dad died. I could be the bear if you don't want to be."

"Terrific. She's alone and heartbroken. What else can go wrong?"

"I don't know. Can I tell my mom you're not a ghost?"

"Sure, kid. Tell her right now."

"Hey mister, you don't look so old anymore."

"That can't be right. You shouldn't see me at all."

"I have good jeans. Mom will be disappointed. She

likes haunted houses."

"Go tell her. Maybe she'll move."

"You just want to sleep some more."

"Yes!"

———◆———

"Mom, I talked to him and he's not a ghost. So what is he?"

"You didn't ask?"

"He doesn't want to play bears."

"That eliminates ghost right there."

"He's been asleep for twelve years."

"Mm-hm."

"He thinks you're still heartbroken over Dad."

"Uh-huh."

"Mom! Pay attention! If he's not a ghost, we have to move again!"

"I hope not. At least you're having fun here."

"You were right, Mom, a farm is the best. It's got millions of places. I want to stay and stay."

"I hope so."

"The ghost won't like it. He wants us to move out so he can sleep."

"I'm sure he does, honey."

"He was old before but now he's getting younger."

"Well, let me know if he turns into a little kid."

———◆———

"You may as well come out. I'm not shutting the door until you do."

<silence>

"You don't have to live in the cellar, you know."

<silence>

"I'm painting the upstairs."

"She's your daughter all right."

"I understand you've been asleep for twelve years."

"So?"

"So you're not a ghost."

"That's your daughter's opinion, too."

"I'm guessing you're a house spirit."

"What's it to you—oh. You want the house painted."

"For starters."

"Wow, you're a lot younger now. Is it because you're in daylight? Ghosts can't be in daylight. Mom says you're a house spirit. That means you get to do things I'm not allowed to do."

"Bully for you, kid."

"Do you hate painting? I love painting."

"Can you paint and talk at the same time?"

"Not very well."

"Here."

"You're letting me paint!"

"Great, now you'll squeal on me to your mom."

"Well she's bound to see it all over me. I paint messy."

"I'll clean you up so she never knows…if you'll shut up."

"That's a bribe. Mom says she is above bribing me."

"Your mom's pants are on fire."

"You're done already! It's beautiful."

"Thanks."

"Was she any trouble?"

"We negotiated a deal."

"Do you eat?"

"Not much."

"I'm a good cook."

"I can smell that."

"C'mon, don't be a grumpy gus. She doesn't talk with her mouth full."

"You've persuaded me."

"Do house spirits eat?"

"If you put a gun to my head. I thought you said she shuts up?"

"Here, watch this."

"Okraaaaa!"

"Why did you stay when the farm was abandoned?"

"Got tired of funerals."

"Everyone was sick here? Oh, dear. What did they die of?"

"Love."

"Seriously, was it contagious?"

"Sadly, it never is."

"But it didn't kill you."

"It never does. Hey, it's working. She shut up."

"Don't change the subject."

"Don't ask me about it and I won't."

"Chickennnnn!"

"She just chows her way through that stuff like a hay baler."

"One course at a time. Her father was like that."

"You miss him?"

"It's been four years."

"You're still running away from him."

"He's dead."

"Doesn't stop people from running."

"Listen, you, I'm running toward, not running away."

"Macaroneeeee!"

"Keep running and you might live."

"So the love that kills won't get me, huh? You must really want us out of here."

"I never said that."

"Pants on fire."

"So how many places have you guys lived?"

"I'm not sure. I was little sometimes."

"Count what you remember."

"First we went to Fort Wayne and there was Alan. Then we went to Cincinnati and there was Brian. Then we went to Peoria and—"

"Lemme guess. Charlie? Cecil? Your mom has a tidy mind."

"Thank you for letting me paint some more."

"Thank you for not telling her. Why a new city every time?"

"I'm not finished. Peoria was Carl. Dave-and-port was Dave."

"You said Dave-and-port."

"Mom told me to stop saying it that way."

"And we see how well that worked. Why a new state every time?"

"They died."

"They what?"

"Died. All gone."

"I can see why you're interested in ghosts."

"She doesn't want ghosts of old boyfriends."

"Just new ones, eh?"

"You were almost a ghost. Why did you get old?"

"Everybody needs love to survive, kid."

"My mom loves me the best of everybody."

"And don't you forget it."

"Are you in love so you can get young?"

"Doesn't work that way, kid."

"Well why do people fall in love?"

"Good question."

"That's a terrible answer. You have to do better than that."

"Look, you, I'll put up with your mouth only so far."

"When Mom says 'Look, you' I know I'm far enough."

"You're so far, you're far out."

"Outa sight."

"I like you, kid. Holy shit, look at your shirt."

"Did you say 'holy shit' to my child?"

"Sue me."

"You live here. You won't leave. Therefore you will watch your language around my child."

"Or what? You'll kill me?"

"You'd have to be in love with me for me to kill you."

"Like Abe and Bob and Chad and Dildo?"

"What did you sa—she told you about them?"

"Next room, I think we'll paint the ceiling first."

"Don't change the subject. I did not—kill—my boyfriends."

"I didn't ask her how far down the alphabet you've got so far."

"Are you threatening me?"

"Hey, my house is made of glass. Ain't throwing

stones."

"They died. Their hearts were broken."

"You break 'em?"

"No, I did not! They were heartbroken when we met! I tried to comfort them and it—it didn't work."

"It never does."

"Well at least I tried!"

"Stop trying."

"Is that what happened to the people who lived here? You tried to—"

"Your kid asked me if I fall in love to get young."

"She doesn't know what house spirits are."

"Do you?"

"Yes. I think I do."

"Better be sure. There's different flavors."

"Well 'bad attitude' seems to be yours."

"Mine's Roumanian."

"You say that like it's a bad thing."

"You're not really a country girl, are you?"

"What's that got to do with it?"

"Simmer down, sheesh. Country girls know about hired hands. Hired hands come in different flavors. You get your good-for-nothing cousin, he's your slave for life but that cuts two ways. You get your local semi-drunk who can't hold down a better job. You get your hobo, he's good for a day but then buh-bye. And once in a while you get a gypsy."

"Is that an ethnic slur? Oh—you're Roumanian. Did you mean Romany?"

"Keep thinking about house spirits."

"Oookay."

"In Roumania we have a house spirit who only comes around when your heart is broken."

"My heart is not broken."

"Anymore. Except for feeling bad about Arnie and Biff and—ow!"

"Why are you such a jerk?"

"So you'll stay at arm's length."

"Back off if you don't want to get slugged!"

"I'm backing, I'm backing."

"Continue. Roumanian house spirits."

"And he's very handy around the house. After a while he even starts to look like the guy who left you."

"Yes, I know."

"You—what? You know?"

"I already knew you were a house spirit. I know stuff."

"So do you know this part? Sooner or later your Roumanian house spirit just can't help comforting your broken heart."

"Not mine."

"All right, someone else's broken heart. Someone who isn't a spiky—as spiky as you."

"Go on."

"And then she dies."

"He kills her."

"He gives her back the love she lost."

"Can't be that good, if she dies of it."

"Oh yes it can."

"Now you're bragging."

"Not exactly. But she forgets to eat. She doesn't sleep. And…"

"You killed them all. All the people who lived here."

"They loved. They lost. I did my job. They died."

"That's heartless."

"I'm not. I hate funerals. That's why I've slept here for twelve years. Very peacefully, might I add, until you and little big mouth showed up."

"You 'did your job.'"

"I am what I am, dammit. What are you? You kill and then you move out of state."

"You bastard!"

"Hit me again and you'll—ow! Hey!"

"If it weren't for my daughter I'd stay and risk prosecution. I don't care if I die! I move so she can still have a mother!"

"And you said you were running toward, not running away."

"Let go of me!"

"Quit hitting. Oof!"

"I'm—looking—"

"Bite me and you'll pay!"

"I'm—looking—for—something—very—specific—don't you manhandle me!"

"Hey! All right, that's enough!"

"Not while I can fight!"

"How far down the alphabet did you get?"

"What?"

"What was the last dead guy's name?"

"Look, you!"

"I wanna know if I'm safe."

"You're hurting my arm."

"You still wanna hit me?"

"His...his name was Kyle."

"Bingo."

<heavy breathing>

"Why? What's your name?"

"I don't have a name. In Roumania we're called lideric."

"Bingo."

<more heavy breathing>

"What?"

"You asked what I'm running toward."

"You're—you mean—"

"I mean I already know about Roumanian house spirits."

"Holy shit."

"I've been following rumors for three years."

"You really do want to die."

"I'm looking for someone I can't kill with love."

"You're—what? How—what makes you—are you—"

"I figure my father was one of those. Before I was born. He ran away and then they think he came back. But it wasn't him. It was one of you."

"I see. Your mother survived? How?"

"The house caught fire while they were—um—and the firemen broke down the door. The man impersonating her husband disappeared."

"Oh."

"He never had time to love her to death."

"Mm."

"And then I was born…half…one of you."

"Huh. Kiss me again."

"Oh, I get to kiss you but not slug you?"

<silence>

"Okay, you are adequate at that."

"Can't get under the telephone wire."

Jennifer Stevenson lives with her husband in Chicago in an old house owned by two cats and haunted by only a few very well-behaved ghosts. Visit her website at www.jenniferstevenson.com and sign up to get announcements about new releases, freebies, deleted scenes, and other fun stuff.

About the Story

I am indebted to Valya Lupescu and Madeline Carol Matz for introduction to their notions of house spirit. I took some liberties with their idea, blended them with a Roumanian sex demon, stirred, popped it all in the oven, and ended up with a Roumanian-American house spirit doing daycare.

Violence Begets...

Paul S. Piper

Logan heard a loud *Pfssssssssttttt!*, a sharp POP, then the engine died.

"God Dammit!" Logan struck the frozen steering wheel with his fist.

"What!?" Kath growled, roused from sleep.

"Car just died!"

"But it's still moving!"

"Shut up!!"

Logan wrenched the frozen wheel to the right using brute strength, easing the car onto a thin gravel shoulder, pumping the nearly useless brake. Outside the night was infinite with stars.

"Fucking power steering and brakes went out. Engine's dead."

"Are we out of gas?"

"No!" He exhaled noisily. "Shut up, Kath. Please?"

The car, a Toyota sedan, stuttered to a halt on the gravel.

"Where the hell are we anyway?"

"Kath, please." Logan shook his head vigorously to get a grip on himself. "Somewhere on the road between Jackson and Dillon."

"Whatever that means," Kath snapped, now alert, sitting up.

"It means no one lives anywhere near here." Logan wiped his mouth with the sleeve of his coat. "It means I haven't passed another car in over an hour, we have a dead car, and we're in the middle of god-damned-nowhere!"

"That's not all that's dead." Kath stuttered a dry laugh.

"Shut up!"

"You should have seen those kids. They were so scared they were going to die."

"Shut up," softer this time.

"And then they did."

Logan could still see the slaughter they'd left in the Victor, Montana farmhouse. A killing spree, the media was calling it. Blood-splattered walls, carpet, furniture. The trail had begun in Mehama, Oregon, continued through the Idaho panhandle, and was now moving through Montana. The exhilaration of the Victor house had faded to fatigue by now, but anger and fear were giving Logan an edge to work with.

"How far are we from there?" Kath asked soberly. "Victor?"

"A hundred miles, maybe more."

They sat there for a moment without talking, the night equally soundless outside the car windows. The car rested in a low saddle scattered with aspen groves, clumps of pine, and meadow, all lit by starlight. The sky seemed to reach down and scrape the earth. A huge, bottomless night sky.

"Fuck," muttered Logan. He popped the hood lever, opened the car door, and stepped out to meet the outer dark. It was cold. He shook his head again and breathed deeply, feeling his heart reckless in his chest.

Far off he heard coyotes yipping, and some strange night-bird. The air smelled of wet grass.

He walked around to the hood and pulled it up, propping it open. There was no light except that of the stars, and the exposed wires, hoses, the engine body with its strange extrusions and cavities, made no sense to Logan. He stared at it and exhaled.

After a few minutes, he reached in and felt the heat on his hands. He began pulling softly at wires, feeling for looseness, a lost connection. He could hear Kath inside the car saying, "Logan? Logan? What are you doing?"

Just then he spotted headlights, still far off, coming from the opposite direction. Kath must have noticed them at the same time, for she scrambled out of the car and came up to him.

"What if it's a cop?" she asked.

"I'll take care of it," Logan said. "Like I always do. Just keep mum." He ducked into the car and retrieved a .38 tucked under the driver's seat, slipping it into his belt, dropping his shirt over it.

The headlights became brighter, and within minutes a pickup truck crossed the center line and pulled to a stop directly in front of the Toyota, blocking its path. Logan heard the engine idle for a spell, then cut. Shortly after, the driver's door opened and a lanky man stepped down. Logan placed him around fifty, his hair short and salty under a battered Stetson cowboy hat. Clean-shaven.

"Problems?" the man said. Logan would have thought the drawl fake if they hadn't been in jack-center of rural Montana ranch country.

"Car died."

"Out of gas?" the man asked.

"No!" Logan wiped his mouth with the back of his hand. "Don't know what it is."

"Mind if I take a look?"

"Be my guest." Logan swept his arm toward the open hood. "It's all Greek to me in there."

"Yeah, these damn modern cars are all computers. Not like the old days. Give me an old Galaxy any day. Something with space and simplicity." The man stepped over and bent down, reaching into the engine cavity, fiddling with this and that.

"You work on cars?"

"Was a mechanic in Dillon."

"Where's that?"

"Right down the road the way you're headed." The man looked up for a moment. "Say, you folks aren't lost, are you? You're a long way from Indiana."

"Indiana?" Logan looked puzzled. "We're coming from Oregon."

"Oh, I just thought, seeing your plates and all."

"Ahh...yeah, those. It's my buddy's car. We just borrowed it for the trip. A little vacation. Me and the wife."

"Oh yeah, didn't see her in there at first. Purty gal."

"Yeah, she is."

Logan shifted from one foot to the other as the man continued to study the situation under the hood.

"You got any tools?" the man asked, pulling his head out from under and standing up. Logan noticed he had a slight hunch to his upper back and shoulders, as if a great weight had borne down on him for a number of years.

"No. No tools."

"That's okay. I've got some in the truck." The man walked back to the truck and opened the passenger door, fishing around behind the seat in the extended cab. He emerged a few seconds later with a gunmetal box of tools and a flashlight. Setting the tools on the ground in front of the Toyota, he waved the flashlight under the hood for a few minutes.

"Mind if I get back into the car?" Logan asked him. "I'm getting cold."

"No problem," the man said, opening the tool box and extracting a socket wrench.

Logan got back into the car and shut the door.

"What is he doing?" Kath hissed.

"He's fixing the fucking car," Logan whispered.

"But he's seen us!"

"I'll take care of it. After he's fixed the car."

"What if he can't?"

"Then I take care of it and we take his truck."

"That's a dumb idea! What if someone recognizes it? He probably lives around here."

"He said he's a mechanic in Dillon."

"Where's that?"

"Just shut up. I said I'll take care of it."

"Just like you took care of..."

"I said shut up." Logan stared out the window into the night and time passed.

Logan woke to a rap at the window, and looked up to see the man standing there. He cracked the door.

"Try it."

Logan turned the key, and after a couple stumbles the motor caught and purred.

"Wow. That's cool. What was wrong?"

"You don't want to know." The man laughed and straightened. "I'm going to take off, leave you folks to your trip."

"Thanks, man! Thanks! Can I offer you some money? It's the least I can do."

"Naw. I get enjoyment out of helping people."

Then the man stuck his hand out and Logan shook it. "Name's Myron. Myron Twisp. You get to Dillon and need anything, you ask around. Lots of people know me. I've lived there all my life."

"Okay, Myron, well, thanks again."

Myron picked up the tool box and walked over to his truck. Logan got out and stretched, walking behind him quietly. While Myron was leaning in returning the tool box to its place behind the seat, Logan slipped the gun out of his belt. The shot ruptured the night, the second coming a split second later.

"Here," he shouted at Kath. "Help me drag him into that ditch."

The man was heavy, but with Logan on one leg and Kath on the other, they managed to pull him across the road and tip him over the edge into a small ravine.

They watched him roll down the busted rock, gathering speed, then crash through some brush that bordered a small stream. Looking again, even with the guy's flashlight, not an inch of his body was visible.

"Get in the driver's seat and follow me."

Kath did as she was told.

Logan drove the pickup slowly, finding a set of tire tracks several hundred yards down the highway. He opened the wire gate, then drove without lights up into an aspen grove, where he left the truck.

"Move over." Kath slid over to the passenger seat.

Logan climbed into the Toyota, turned the car around, and drove back down the road to the gate, refastening it. He looked up at the hillside, studying the aspen grove, but the truck was invisible. Then he got back into the car, turned it down the highway, and headed toward Dillon. The night and its billion stars were the only witnesses.

Logan sat at the bar in a downtown place called The Dusty Nail sipping a cold long-neck. He'd left Kath at the motel, just having to get out. She was blah-blah-blahing him into the ground with her endless reiterations of the last slaughter, particularly of what she did to the children, how she did it, how they screamed and begged. Doing it was one thing, and he'd been there and felt the vast release, the exhilaration, but it was fucked up to feed on it for days. They needed another kill.

He watched a long-haired guy, mid-late forties, enter the bar and futz with the jukebox. Some nameless country song emerged from the ancient speaker, and the guy headed over to the bar, taking a seat one away from Logan. He signaled the bartender, who walked over.

"Bert. How ya doing?"

"Thirsty, Russell. How 'bout a Coors?"

"Sure thing. How's the cow business?"

"'Bout like it always is. Moving 'em up to higher ground."

"Over by Lima Creek?"

"There, and up Alden."

The bartender, Russell, walked off to get Bert's beer. Logan noticed he limped, favoring his left foot. Bert must have noticed Logan studying the bartender because he said, "He used to ride rodeo till a bull fell on his leg."

Logan turned to study the man. He had a narrow, weathered face, hair the color of straw, cool blue eyes.

"You new here?" the cowboy asked. "Haven't seen you around before."

"Just passing through."

"It's a good town to do that." Russell set the beer in front of Bert, who thanked him, then took a sip and turned back to Logan. "Where you headed?"

"Down to Idaho for now. Idaho Falls maybe."

"That's easy enough to do. Just turn south on 15

and press down on the gas. Take my advice and don't look back."

"You grow up here?" Logan asked.

"Unfortunately, yes. It's a random world. I could just as easily have been born rich on the Upper East Side."

"Where's that?" Logan asked.

"New York City," replied Bert. "It's where my damn cousins live."

"Huh."

They drank in silence for a few minutes, Bert humming along to the jukebox song he'd chosen.

"Say, you've lived here awhile. You must know everyone. You know a guy named Myron Twisp? A mechanic?"

Bert gave him a strange look. "You haven't met Myron, have you?'

"Nah. A guy in Great Falls told me to look him up if I was down this way. Said he has a way with a wrench, and the car's been giving me and the little lady some problems."

Bert continued to stare at Logan, which was beginning to piss him off.

Then Bert said, quietly, "Myron Twisp is dead. Died over twenty years ago."

Logan whistled. "I'll be damned." Then he smiled, weakly. "My friend didn't mention that."

"You didn't break down out there, did you? Myron drove up in his truck to help?"

Logan felt himself turning white, fought for control.

"Just like I said, this buddy of mine…"

"Myron was a killer. But, different." The cowboy scratched his nose. "You hear of a TV show called *Dexter*?"

"Nah. Don't watch TV much."

"Well, Dexter was a serial killer, but he only killed other serial killers. Dig?"

"Yeah, I guess." Logan tipped his beer, not realizing it was empty. He set it down carefully, studying his arm and hand to make sure they weren't shaking.

"Myron was like that. He traveled the state, and several others, killing people. He had this thing about people who abused or hurt little kids. Turns out he'd been abused pretty bad when he was little. Kind of a vengeance thing. 'Course we didn't find out any of this till Myron killed himself. The sheriff found a bunch of evidence. Photos, a journal, notes. They started putting together all the pieces, and found out Myron was really doing society a great service. Cutting out cancers, you might say."

"Huh."

"Crazy thing was, he always used a hatchet. 'Course the press called him an axe murderer, but that's just the press. Making it more dramatic."

"Huh," Logan said again, wanting another drink badly, but frozen, unable to order one. "When did he kill himself?" he finally asked.

"Like I said. Around twenty years ago."

Logan finally summoned up enough courage to signal the bartender, who limped over.

"Give me another one of these, and a double shot of Jack Black."

"Funny thing is," Bert continued, "he's still out there."

"What do you mean?"

"He's still killing people. Child molesters and abusers. Only now he's a ghost."

"A ghost!? That's crazy. I don't believe in ghosts." Logan knew the man he'd shot next to his truck, the man he and Kath had dragged over to the edge and toppled down that ravine, was no ghost. That man was flesh and blood and bone.

"You don't have to believe. Don't make any difference. And as long as you mind your business, don't hurt no little kids, there's no problem." The cowboy laughed, threw a ten on the bar and stood up.

Logan was nervously peeling the label from his beer.

"Take care, stranger. Safe travels." Bert turned to the bartender who was walking the drinks over to Logan, gave him a mock salute.

"Bye, Russ," he said, and walked out of the bar.

Logan watched the door swing shut behind him, then neatly, carefully, picked up the shot of whiskey and downed it, chasing it with the beer. He had three more of these before he threw two twenties on the bar and staggered out into the night.

The light was on in the motel room when he opened the door, and Kath sat in the pull-out chair at the small desk, her iPad open, the screen-saver flickering colors, and a hatchet cleaving her head nearly in two. Logan shut the door quick, and scanned the room. There was a tiny closet and the bathroom. He slipped the pistol into his hand and did a quick search. Nothing. Blood had splattered the walls near where Kath sat dead, and Logan imagined the force behind the hatchet was powerful. Blood still flowed weakly from the wound, following the contours of Kath's body to the cheap brown shag carpet where it staled.

Logan acted quickly and without thinking much. He stuffed the few clothes they'd extracted back into the black suitcase, grabbed his bathroom bag, and exited the room. Examining the parking lot and the street in front, he saw nothing unusual. Tossing the clothes and the bathroom bag into the back seat, he opened the trunk and dropped the suitcase in, slamming the trunk shut. The night was the same as last night—vast and teeming with stars. The only witness, he thought, to what had happened, to what would happen next.

Then suddenly he knew what he needed to do.

This whole thing was a setup. Somehow that guy at the bar, Bert, had found out what happened, who he and Kath were. Logan didn't know how this had happened, but it was the only answer. And the guy Myron that he'd shot, had lived, and crawled out of that ravine, retrieved his truck, and made it back to town. Hell, Bert was probably his best friend. He was probably at Bert's right now, nursing himself back to health. Ghost, my ass!

Logan drove like an idiot, running on adrenaline and booze. He covered the distance back to where they'd dumped the body. Slamming on the brakes, he jumped out and bolted over the edge, glissading scree down the steep bank, plunging wildly into the brush where the body had lain. A few seconds, and he'd have the answer. Then he'd drive back to Dillon and hunt down Bert and his friend Myron.

But the body was still there, and the starlight painted it cold.

Logan felt a spasm of shivering overtake him, and the sounds that ruptured from his throat were barely human. But the night swallowed them, and finally he had enough strength and coordination to scramble up out of the ravine and climb back into the car. He sat there still shivering erratically. There was no sense in checking for the truck. He needed to get the hell out of here. He'd head back toward Dillon, then hook a right south on 15 and make for Idaho Falls.

He started the car and swung it into a U-turn,

jamming his foot down on the gas. There was a mile-long straightaway as the road crossed a narrow valley, then began a series of curves as it headed downhill to Dillon. It was toward the end of this straightaway that Logan sensed movement, and he glanced into the rearview mirror and saw the face of the dead man he'd just left in the ravine, smiling, and then saw the hatchet crash down on his skull, felt the staggering blow, the car leave the road, and as it tipped sideways, saw the night sky full of stars, their cold light bearing witness yet again.

Paul S. Piper was born in Chicago a long time ago, lived for extensive periods in Montana, Hawaii, and the PNW. A retired librarian, he's turned his life over to writing, traveling, and leisure. Paul has five published books of poetry, including *Dogs and Other Poems* (featured by Ted Kooser's *American Life in Poetry*), contributed to numerous anthologies, and co-edited several books of essays. His fiction largely explores the effect of politics and/or technology on nature. His novel *The Wolves of Mirr* was recently published by Book View Café.

About the story

There are stretches of deserted highway in Montana, that driven at night, will make a believer out of anyone in ghosts, UFOs, bigfeet, werewolves, or whatever night terrors are imaginable. I chose a particularly ghostly stretch of highway between Wisdom and Dillon, Montana to set my story. High sage-land, with dense patches of forest, and at almost 6,000 feet in altitude, seems to graze the sky. The theme of my story is an old one—a man stops to help a stranger with car trouble, fixes the car, and later in town the stranger discovers the helper has been dead for years. I took this meme and gave it a twist. Montana has few lawmen, and occasionally killers roam freely, evading escape for years, or possibly forever. Furthermore, I enjoy stories where a character assumes they are in control, only to realize, too late, that someone else holds the puppet strings.

The Nature of Things

Maya Kaathryn Bohnhoff

"Can someone explain to me what a box labeled 'cookware' is doing in the upstairs guest bath?"

Harry Ferguson looked up from the laptop perched atop the kitchen table to see his wife, Marilyn, standing in the kitchen archway rooting in her purse for her keys.

Across the table from Harry, his teenaged daughter, Kim, looked up from her last bite of Rice Krispies. "I didn't do it."

"Don't look at me." Her younger brother, Scott, had already deposited his dishes in the sink.

"Gosh," said Marilyn, still rooting. "Must've been those darned cookware fairies. Harry, honey, if you could move it back down... Oh, here they are." Marilyn produced her car keys with a flourish. "I'm off. In the car, kids."

Scott was already out the door with the delicate patter of size eleven sneakers. His sister followed at a more decorous pace.

"Sure you'll be okay here with Megan?" Marilyn asked Harry. "What if you have to go to the office?"

"I'll just take Meg with me. Gwen loves her."

"Hm. How does the DA feel about it?"

"He'll love anything that contributes to the prosecution of a case, even if it involves a five-year-old in the law library. He might even hire her. After all, she knows everything."

Marilyn laughed and kissed his cheek. "Good luck."

Good luck. He'd need it, he mused over his coffee. It was a bad time to have moved into a new house, but moving was always a pain in the wazoo, and the real-estate market did not obey human whim.

Which made his personal and professional life a matched set; the case he was working on was equally disobedient. They had a body—Marcellus Boite, owner of a downtown gun shop. They had a suspect—Ernest Combs, a small-time embezzler Boite had had the misfortune to hire. They had a motive—Boite had recently reported to the police that some inventory was missing. They had opportunity—Combs had no alibi for the time of his employer's death. They had suspicious behavior—confronted with a police presence, Combs fled, though he claimed an emergency at home.

What they did not have was a murder weapon.

Boite had died of a single .38 caliber bullet to the head, but no gun had been found during the search of Combs's home and car, and no record existed that he had ever owned one. Till now, he'd been a "numbers" man—mangling accounts, not people; his thefts had been confined to the virtual world. His fingerprints were everywhere at the crime scene, but then he worked there. The only place they mattered was on the conspicuously absent murder weapon.

Harry grimaced at the taste of his coffee and went to the fridge for milk. The carton was empty.

"Damn." He was in the act of putting the carton back when he caught himself and sheepishly threw it in the trash.

Returning to his makeshift workspace, he read Combs's criminal record again, slowly. A tiny sound from the foyer made him glance up expecting to see Meg. The words "How're you feeling, sweetie" stalled on his lips when he realized there was no one there.

"Winslow, leave the ficus alone!"

There was a rustle of foliage and the soft thump of little cat feet. Harry went back to the futile task of trying to pry leads out of Combs's file.

Ernest Combs was a man without a life. A man who could be reduced to a birth date, a list of schools, a series of dead-end jobs, and a succession of unspectacular crimes. Maybe, Harry thought, he'd committed murder out of boredom, figuring that prison *had* to be more stimulating than life on the outside.

The rustle of ficus leaves repeated. Without raising his head, Harry said, "Winslow! You're cruisin' for a bruisin'."

"What's that mean?"

Harry jumped. His youngest daughter stood in the foyer, still in her PJs, a stuffed Pooh bear tucked under one arm.

"Hi, sweetie," he said, wondering what had made him think he could work at home. "Feeling better?"

"I'm hungry," she announced and flounced into the kitchen to pull herself up into a chair across from him.

He wasn't getting anywhere with Ernest Combs anyway. He rose and began a search for breakfast cereal. "Glad to hear it. What'll it be?"

"Scrambledy eggs. *Please*, Daddy?"

He made the mistake of looking at her. The sweet heart-shaped face with its chocolaty brown eyes, the silky auburn hair, tousled from sleep. Her Pooh bear smiled amiably at him from under her chin.

"As you wish. If I can find the cookware."

They'd been in the house for about a week and had yet to cook. They'd unpacked cereal bowls and flatware and little else. Nothing was where it belonged, every available corner was piled with boxes, the furniture was half-arranged. As were Harry's thoughts. He felt guilty for not unpacking, but knew if he unpacked, the guilt of not working on the case would be just as intense.

Belatedly, Harry recalled that the cookware box was in the upstairs bathroom. He dragged it down to the kitchen, popped the lid, and rummaged for a sauté pan.

"Daddy? What sort of animal lives in a closet?"

Goody, Harry thought, *a five-year-old joke.* "I give, honey, what lives in a closet?"

"*Dad*-dy," she said in a tone of voice that suggested he had slightly less wattage than an oven light.

The phone rang and he leapt to get it before the voicemail kicked in, giving Megan the universal shush sign, finger to lips. "Ferguson's."

"We may have a problem," his assistant, Gwen, said without preamble. "We've got two weeks to build a case. Not four."

"How did that happen?"

"Fortis pled personal duress. Her baby is due in a month and a half. She told the judge it might be early. Which is such bull. Merle Fortis has delivered two weeks late three times running. And, if that's not bad enough, the date change lands us with a different judge: 'Technicality' Quinn."

Harry rolled his eyes. Justice Erica Quinn had earned her nickname for an unparalleled record of throwing cases out on technicalities.

"Yeah, I know," Gwen said, as if she had heard his eyes turning in their sockets. "I have some case law for you, counselor. I know Meg's not well, and I'd bring it to you, but John's got me on the Edwards case. I'm not even getting a lunch break."

"Meg's well enough to ride in the car."

"Great. I'll leave the stuff on your desk."

Harry rang off, his mind tilting slightly at the thought of trying to mount this case in two weeks. His eyes went unfocused to the *ficus benjamina* by the front door. It seemed to have blossomed. A bright red sock was cradled among the leaves.

Damned cat. He retrieved the sock and shook out the ficus debris. A "watched" feeling made his nape hairs prickle; he turned to find Winslow regarding him quizzically from the middle of the staircase. A strange creature whose behavior was less than catlike, Winslow followed his favorite human everywhere. He allowed himself to be led on a leash. He fetched. He stole socks.

Harry shook the sock at him. "Winslow, I'm sorry we haven't found your cat toys, but..." He knew a moment of guilt as the tabby's dark yellow eyes gazed back at him, soulful and doggish. He decided he'd buy a catnip mouse today. A red one.

"Hey, Meg, honey, how about breakfast at Applebee's?"

"Fortis will move for dismissal due to insufficient evidence." Those were the first words out of Gwen's mouth when Harry entered the office. She smiled when she saw Megan standing in the doorway behind him. "Hi, sweetie. How're you feeling?"

"My nose is sniffly." She demonstrated.

"The case law?" Harry prompted.

Gwen ignored him. "Poor baby. Want a tissue?" She snatched one from the box on her desk.

"Gwen, the case law?"

"Oh, yeah. Here." She moved to his desk and bent

to embrace a stack of legal books. A rainbow of little vinyl tags sprouted festively from the pages.

"The blue ones," Gwen said, "are cases in which the defendant worked for the victim. The red ones deal with search and seizure powers. In the yellow ones the defendant skipped bail. Purely cautionary."

"Any of them give you gooseflesh?"

Gwen swore that when she encountered items that "meant something" she felt as if someone were blowing on the back of her neck.

"Anderson vs. the State of California," she said, then added, "Want me to show you how to use that tissue, sweetie?" She was smiling past Harry at Megan who was snuffling into Pooh's ear.

Gwen, he thought, *is a mother waiting to happen.* "I can arrange for you to borrow her."

"Hah. Go study your case law, counselor."

Homeward bound, Harry was jarred out of his ruminations by an irregular thudding on the back of his car seat. "Meg, please stop that."

The thudding was replaced by steady pressure.

"Megan! Stop kicking my seat." He glanced up into the rearview mirror, half expecting to catch an urchin grin; she was gazing out the window.

She faced forward. "I *wasn't* kicking your seat, Daddy."

"You were pushing it with your feet."

"No, I wasn't."

"Meg."

"I *wasn't.*"

He pulled the car into the driveway contemplating how to handle the fib. "Look, honey. I realize I wasn't paying as much attention to you as I should have at breakfast. But you really need to refrain from these little demonstrations of—"

"What's 'refrain'?"

"Never mind."

"Can I watch TV, Daddy?" Megan asked as they came through the front door.

Harry tripped over a pair of shoes left smack in the middle of the entry and hopped forward, trying not to topple over.

Meg giggled. "You look like a kangaroo."

"Thanks. Yes, you may watch TV." Chances were, she'd fall asleep and he would get some work done... and he wouldn't have to enforce naptime.

Harry went back to the kitchen—noting with annoyance that he'd forgotten to turn off the lights—and started weeding through the case law. As Gwen predicted, he found Anderson vs. the State of California interesting. Because the prime suspect had worked for the victim and the crime had occurred in the workplace, the judge had extended the search warrant to the home of the suspect's ex-wife, which was between his office and home. There they'd found the murder weapon.

Combs didn't have an ex-wife, or even a girlfriend. But the scenario of him dumping the weapon between work and home seemed plausible. The police had gotten to Combs's house within thirty seconds of his arrival, surprising him as he came out of his kitchen. He'd had no time to hide a weapon. Yet no weapon had been found.

Harry went over the timeline: Mrs. Boite called 911; the arresting officers spotted Combs's car less than a half-mile from the crime scene and tailed him back to his house. They'd lost sight of him for about twenty seconds when he ran a light. He'd had no time to take a detour. If he dropped the gun somewhere, it had to be in a direct path between the crime scene and his house.

Harry checked Combs's phone records. Prior to the murder, he'd called only two numbers with addresses in the target area. Ignoring the stentorian falsetto of Muppets filtering in from the living room, Harry emailed the numbers to the lead detective, tagged "urgent." Then he wandered the house, thinking, turning off lights, straightening pictures, moving things from one place to another. He mulled over Ernest Combs as he tsked over the state of the upstairs bathroom, wondering why a row of hair clips marched across the top of the toilet tank.

Combs had a motive.

He dumped the hair clips into a drawer.

Of course, it was a motive that worked for a number of people, including the victim's wife.

Combs had opportunity.

He moved mouthwash from the floor to the medicine cabinet.

Closing the cabinet, he caught movement in the mirror—someone passing the open bathroom door. Meg was too small for him to see more than the top of her head in the bathroom mirror.

He poked his head out into the hall. There was no one there. He started down the hall toward the master bedroom. An inhuman shriek greeted him at the door and Winslow shot out into the hall like a furry cannon ball. He ricocheted off Harry's knees, and skidded toward the staircase.

Heart pounding, Harry teetered on the bedroom threshold with the eerie feeling there was someone standing behind the half-open door. He sucked in a breath and barged into the room, slamming the door against the wall. No one was behind the door.

Harry shook his head, clucking ruefully at himself. He was as bad as Winslow—jumping at shadows. *Dufus.*

The phone rang, drawing him downstairs.

"Checked those numbers," Gwen told him. "Both businesses. A pizza place and a pawnshop."

"Pawnshop? Okay, let's get—"

"Done," Gwen said. "Detectives Price and Kirwan are on it even as we speak. If that's not where Combs disposed of the weapon, maybe it's where he purchased it. You coming to work tomorrow?"

"That's the plan. Marilyn got another professor to cover for her. I can't wait to get back. A half-moved-into house is…damned distracting."

As he rang off, the cartoon voices from the living room cut off in mid-squeak. "Daddy, Winslow and I are gonna take a nap."

He turned to find Meg standing in the foyer with the cat draped over one arm, looking singularly more relaxed than it had the last time he'd seen it. Meg padded upstairs and Harry went back to his case. He was deeply engrossed when he got an email from Detective Price announcing that the pawnshop was a dead end. The owner, Bill Greeley by name, recognized Combs, but had never sold him anything. He'd done a background check on Combs the first time he tried to buy something, uncovered his criminal record, and refused service.

Which didn't keep Combs from trying. He denied that Combs had ever tried to sell him anything.

So, Combs didn't get the gun at the pawnshop nor, if the owner was to be believed, did he dump it there. Then…Harry called up a manifest of Boite's missing inventory. What better place for Combs to arm himself than his employer's stock? Combs's harassment of the pawnshop owner might just be a means of covering his ass.

"All *right*." Harry leaned closer to the screen. There were indeed a number of .38 caliber guns missing—five Smith and Wessons, two Colts, and a couple of Glocks.

Harry's train of thought was derailed by what sounded like a police chase being conducted at warp speed by chipmunks. "Meg, turn that down!"

The cacophony continued. Harry popped up from the table and crossed the foyer to the living room. "Meg, I asked—" He stopped. The TV blared toons into an empty room. He turned off the TV and went upstairs where he found Meg fast asleep on her bed, Winslow sitting Sphinx-like at her feet.

"I gotta get back to the office," Harry told the cat, who yawned.

Downstairs, the front door opened. "Dammit, Harry—you left your shoes in the middle of the entry!"

Harry had left his shoes neatly on the mat behind the ficus, but decided to let it go. He was sincerely glad Marilyn was home, because it meant he could remand stewardship of the house to her, recover his wits, and get to work.

"So now you know Combs had a weapon, right?" Marilyn asked as she settled under the covers.

"*If* he's the one who stole the guns, yeah. The murder weapon was a .38—probably a Smith and Wesson. That narrows it down to five guns in Boite's missing inventory. *If* the murder weapon came from Boite's inventory."

"But?"

"*But* if we don't find the gun, Combs may walk."

"Bummer."

"Meg's going to school tomorrow, right?" Harry asked, yawning.

"I'd rather keep her home one more day, but I've

got it covered. You can return to work, counselor."

"God bless you," Harry murmured. "This house is…creepy."

"What?"

Reality began to recede toward sleep. "Shoes," he mumbled.

"Daddy? *Dad*-dy!" Meg was a blur in the dim light. "Daddy, something's under my bed. Make it go away."

Like a well-trained dog, he rose, trailed her docilely to her room, and looked under her bed. "Nothing there, Muffin."

"I bet he went back into the closet."

He straightened. "Oh. Do you want me to chase him away?"

"No, I don't mind him being there. I just don't like it when he crawls under my bed. He wakes me up."

"Okay. Well, um, you stay in that closet then, you hear?" he said to the half-closed door.

Meg beamed. "Thanks, Daddy."

The next morning, Harry packed his briefcase and escaped the house gleefully, leaving Marilyn in charge. He piled the two older kids into the car and ferried them to school, absently pondering the connection between Combs and the pawnshop; wondering if there wasn't more there than met the eye. Maybe…

"Hey, Scott. Stop kneeing me in the back."

"Huh?"

"You're pushing on the back of my seat," Harry complained, pulling into the turnaround in front of the high school.

Kim shot a grin back at her brother as she opened her door. "Busted. See ya, Dad."

"I *wasn't* pushing on your seat," Scott said. His door slammed.

"Yeah, right," Harry muttered. "Nobody kicks my seat. Nobody leaves the TV on, or the bathroom lights, or the water. Nobody leaves shoes lying in the entry."

He pulled away from the school trying to regain his concentration. Was the pawnshop owner witness or accomplice? If Combs was ripping off his boss, the guns had to go somewhere. It might be productive to bring the guy in...

"Dammit, Scott, I said *stop!*" Harry's annoyance guttered in the realization that Scott was on his way to Algebra 101. He pulled over against the curb and craned his neck around to peer down the back of the seat, expecting to find that Winslow had snuck into the car.

No Winslow.

Great. Now I'm having back spasms.

By the time he stepped out of the elevator into the DA's office, Harry was much more chipper. He had a hunch. He told Gwen as much the moment he entered the office.

"You hide it so well," she said, straight-faced.

Not long after, Harry found himself behind a two-way mirror in an interrogation room watching Detectives Price and Kirwan question Bill Greeley, pawnshop owner. Greeley stuck doggedly to the claim that he knew Ernest Combs only as a nuisance who continued to try to buy weapons and ammo he wouldn't sell him.

"I'm a law-abiding American citizen, dammit," Greeley said for the fiftieth time. "A card-carrying member of the NRA and Neighborhood Watch. I don't sell guns to criminals. Ernest Combs was a criminal."

Detective Price looked into the two-way, rolled his eyes, and mouthed "No go" to the invisible Harry.

"I think he's being straight," Price said later. "The way his eyes bugged out when we asked if he'd purchased arms from Combs, I thought he was going to have a coronary."

"Maybe he's a good actor," Harry said.

"Yeah, but Combs isn't. Practically the first thing he said when the question of gun ownership came up was, 'I can't *buy* a gun in this freakin' town. I tried.' Maybe he was planning all along to use this guy as a sort of alibi—you know, establish that he'd made repeated attempts to buy a gun and failed."

"I still think that gun is hidden somewhere on his property," said Detective Kirwan. "We mentioned that we'd interviewed Greeley. He seemed completely unconcerned, then asked if we'd finished tossing his house. Said we'd better have put everything back where we found it. Said he'd hold us responsible if there was any damage to the place. He seemed a little angsty about it."

"Chitra, we've turned that whole damn place over," argued Price. "The gun's not there."

Harry chewed his lip. "He was exiting the kitchen when the arresting officers entered the house."

The detectives nodded.

"So they started the search there."

"We dismantled the kitchen," Price said, "pulled appliances out from the wall, even looked for hidden compartments."

Kirwan added, "First, we thought it was in the broiler pan because the door was slightly ajar—and stuck, as if it had been closed in a big hurry. Maybe he started to stash the gun there, then changed his mind. Maybe it was a deke."

"He didn't have time to change his mind,"

objected Price. "And why bother with misdirection? We searched everywhere."

"Was he nervous about the search?"

"Yeah, he was. But apparently he didn't need to be."

After lunch Harry paid a visit to Combs's house. It wasn't much more than a shoebox with a peaked roof, but it had obviously just been through a major remodel. Combs had moved in a scant three months before. There were three rooms downstairs: living room, kitchen, bath. The furnishings were simple but tasteful. And they were of a quality beyond the means of most store clerks. There was a hand-knotted silk Persian carpet. The kitchen had Viking appliances.

Suppressing envy, Harry checked the broiler tray, the lettuce crisper, and the garbage disposal, knowing the detectives had already done that. Then he moved to the second floor.

Up a flight of spiral stairs he was confronted by a single, long room with a sharply peaked ceiling that ran the length of the house from front to back. The bed was cherry wood, with side table and dresser to match. A wardrobe stood at the end of the room opposite the door. A wood-burning stove hunkered halfway between in a wide gable, its pipe extending up into the ceiling. Ashes littered the floor in front of it, a souvenir of the police search. Every drawer and cabinet hung open.

Harry had *bubkes*. No clues, no epiphanies, not even a niggle. He went home to the joys of unpacking.

"Any idea where the cookware went?" Marilyn followed her voice into the foyer. "I'd swear it was right here by the table this morning."

"It was. I brought it down myself." Harry mounted the staircase, intent on a quick change into a sweat suit.

"Huh… By the way, you left every light on downstairs this morning."

He stopped halfway up the stairs. "No, I didn't. I only left the foyer light on."

"Oh. Must've been Scott."

"Wasn't me." Scott's voice floated from the living room on a raft of video game sound effects.

Marilyn gestured "never mind" and headed back into the kitchen. "If I can't find the cookware there'll be no dinner tonight—unless you want to order out."

"Pizza!" yelled Scott.

At the top of the stairs, Harry nearly collided with Kim who'd appeared on the landing cradling a box.

"Cookware?"

Kim nodded. "It was in the upstairs bathroom."

"Again? I brought it downstairs," said Harry.

"Sure, Dad." Kim gave him an indulgent smile, then carried the box downstairs.

Marilyn had come out of the kitchen again. She winked up at Harry. "Poltergeists. They also got Scott's homework." When Harry didn't laugh, she followed him up to their bedroom. "No breakthroughs on the case?"

"No." He sat heavily on the bed, shaking his head. "That gun has got to be in Combs's kitchen. He flat-out didn't have time to hide it anywhere else."

"But they searched the whole house."

"Thoroughly."

"Yeah? How about the turkey carcass left over from Thanksgiving?"

Harry smiled. "Checked it. No gun."

Harry Ferguson had long been accused of living in his head. At the moment his head contained an exact replica of the floor plan of Ernest Combs's house. As he padded down his own staircase to let the cat out, he recalled how many steps were in Combs's. Returning upstairs, he was disoriented by the sight of a transverse hallway instead of a right angle turn into a loft.

"Daddy?" Megan's voice issued tentatively from the semi-darkness of her room.

He crossed to her door. "You're supposed to be asleep."

She was sitting up in bed, hands in her lap, watching him solemnly. "I need you to talk to him again. He won't obey me."

"Who, honey?"

"The thing in my closet. He keeps going under my bed. He snores."

Harry smiled. "He snores."

She nodded.

"Okay." Harry crossed to the closet and opened the door quickly, as if he expected to surprise something out of hiding.

Meg cleared her throat delicately. "He's under the *bed*, Daddy."

"Oh, right."

Harry got down on hands and knees and peered beneath the bed. His eyes locked on a darker patch of dark that seemed to be blocking the glow of Meg's nightlight. A frisson ran up his spine before he could chide himself for being over-imaginative. Had to be a stuffed animal. He started to reach under the bed for it and was vaguely ashamed when his hand refused to move.

"You there," he said, making his voice menacingly deep. "You're upsetting my little girl. I must ask you to stop hiding under her bed. Please return to the closet."

He straightened and looked at Meg. "Okay?"

"Thank you, Daddy. You sounded mean. But could you check and make sure he's gone?"

"Oh...sure." He peered beneath the bed again. Odd. Now he could see the nightlight through the bed skirt. He straightened. "Gone."

Meg smiled and held out her arms. "Thanks, Daddy. You're great."

He hugged her. "Glad you think so."

He passed the closet on his way out, half of a mind to open the door and peek. He didn't.

Saturday morning Harry realized he'd dreamed about Combs's house all night. Waking in his flat-ceilinged, perfectly square bedroom was disconcerting.

After breakfast the family dispersed and the house, empty and quiet, seemed to give up a huge sigh. As did Harry. He sat at the kitchen table for a while, savoring his coffee and mulling over the case...for all the good it did.

Coffee exhausted, he wandered upstairs and found every light on. He made a complete round, shutting them off—bathroom, Meg's room, Kim's room, Scott's room, the master bedroom. Then he headed back toward the staircase determined to do some gardening.

The bathroom light was on. Again. He remembered turning it off.

He approached the room cautiously, nape hair at attention. The door was ajar, and he swore he saw movement through the slit between door and jamb. He slapped himself mentally. It was probably an electrical problem. Even new houses could have electrical problems.

He stood uncertainly in the doorway. Then,

swearing under his breath, he thrust the door open. It impacted the wall with a padded thump.

Harry entered the room fully, turned, and swung the door shut, belatedly considering what he'd do if there were someone there. It closed with a swish and flap of the bathrobes hanging on the back.

Harry chuckled. *Alarmist.* He let the door swing half-open and turned his attention to the light switch. It was in the "on" position. He flipped it on and off, then wiggled it. Out of the corner of his eye he saw a shadow slip past the bathroom door and down the hallway. He lunged at the door and flung it open.

Nothing.

He took a deep breath and stepped into the hall, looking both ways and wondering if stress caused hallucinations. Shaking his head, he turned and nudged open the bathroom door.

A thin, dark, little man with startlingly pale, protuberant eyes blinked up at him. He was wearing black pants and a matching long-sleeved turtleneck sweater. He looked like a mime who'd forgotten his makeup.

"Nuts," he said in a high, nasal voice.

An understatement.

"What…what are you doing in my house?" Harry asked around the lump in his throat.

"Ex-*cuse* me. This is really embarrassing."

"What are you doing in my house?" Harry repeated.

"Uh…I work here."

"Who *are* you?"

"I'm the Thing That Hides Behind Doors. Did I scare you?"

"Hell, yes! I thought I was going to turn around and find you sneaking up behind me."

"Oh, not *me*. That would be the Thing That Sneaks

Up Behind You. He's off today. Now, if you'll excuse me..." He started to turn away.

"No, I won't excuse you! You *work* here?"

"Yessir. Really, I oughta get going. I'm not supposed to talk to you. Wow. This is weird."

"No kidding." Harry's heart rate slowed. The guy didn't seem dangerous, just incoherent and nervous. "Who are you?"

"Didn't I say? I'm the Thing That—"

"Hides Behind Doors. I caught that. I just don't know what it means."

The guy fidgeted, his big watery eyes bobbing this way and that. "It means...well, pretty much what it says. I hide behind doors. I'm a—a Thing."

"A thing..." Harry shook his head. "What do you mean 'a thing'?"

The protuberant eyes flicked back to Harry's face. "I really shouldn't be talking to you. Can I go now?"

"Go? I find you in my bathroom and I'm supposed to just let you go?"

"Aw, c'mon. I promise to do better. Only don't tell the Boss."

"How about the police?"

He seemed puzzled. "The police? What would the police care? This isn't their jurisdiction...is it?"

"I'm willing to find out." Harry stepped backwards into the hall.

The little fellow quivered and glanced feverishly about. "Oh, *jeez*, mister. I don't want—" His eyes darted to a spot over Harry's left shoulder and froze there. "Oops."

Harry swung around. A tall, thin, sepulchral fellow faced him across the upstairs runner. He wore a black serge suit with a long coat and string tie. Sad, dark eyes were a perfect match for the doleful set of his mouth, while graying eyebrows arched toward a distant hairline. The man inclined his head.

Harry dropped into a posture he'd seen in a Jackie Chan movie. "Stay back. I know Kung Fu."

"Of course you do, sir. But I came only to apologize."

"Apologize..."

"For the behavior of my staff."

"Your staff?" Harry realized he was echoing, but could think of nothing remotely intelligent to say.

"The Household Things. I am, I regret to say, the Chief Thing for this domicile. I am forced to admit, sir, that in all my years in your service, I have never had such a raw and undisciplined crew."

"You've...you've been in my service," Harry echoed, "for years."

"Well, not your service precisely, sir, but your family's. In fact, I've been in service to this family since you married and rented that quaint little cottage on Sepulveda." He said "quaint" with the same disdain Scott showed when he said "peas." "Your personal staff are quite good, if I do say so myself, but these other Things..." The sad eyes rolled heavenward.

"What do you mean 'things'? What *things*?"

"Well, sir, since you inquired—there are three classes of Things in your service. Personal Things (which include myself and immediate staff), Furnishings Things, and of course Household Things such as the Thing That Hides Behind Doors." Contempt curled his thin lips. "It is the last group that has caused the trouble, I fear. They are inexperienced and cocky, which I suspect comes with attachment to one of these 'designer' homes. Modern conveniences, indeed."

"They've caused trouble?"

"Oh, sir, surely you've noticed how clumsy they are. Never waiting long enough to turn on lights you've turned off; open doors you've closed; close doors you've opened. And they are too ambitious altogether. Why, the Thing That Lurks in the Closet of your youngest daughter's room has been bucking for a promotion to Thing That Hides Under the Bed since you moved in. He's disturbed the dear child a number of times. No, I fear your Household Things are utterly without experience and poorly trained."

"P-poorly trained?"

"Especially in comparison with your Personal and Furnishings crews."

"Ah," Harry said, as if he understood one word of what this odd man was telling him. "Those crews are...more experienced and better trained, then."

The funereal fellow drew himself up to his full height, reminding Harry of Jeeves, the quintessential butler. "I pride myself on it, sir. As I said, your Personal Things have been with your family since your first rental. And even your Furnishings Things have been with you long enough to understand your comings and goings—with the possible exception of the Thing that came with your new car."

"A Thing came with my *car*?"

"Yes sir. The Thing That Kicks the Driver's Seat. He's the newest member of the crew. But I have confidence that in a few weeks' time, he'll get the hang of it."

"M-my car has a Thing."

"Yes sir. As do all your major appliances."

"Appliances...as in our washing machine and dryer?"

"The Thing That Hides Socks."

"Our refrigerator?"

"The Thing That Drinks the Last of the Milk and Puts the Carton Back Empty."

"I thought that was my *son*."

Jeeves beamed. "As you were meant to, sir."

"Is there a Thing That Feeds Pâté to the Cat?"

"That would be your youngest daughter. You also have a Thing That Rumples the Carpets. In some homes he would also do bedspreads, but you have a cat for that purpose. Cats are honorary Things," he added.

Harry rubbed his temples. "You and your staff work at *scaring* us?"

"Oh, *no* sir. Our purpose is to *engage* you, keep you on your toes, make your lives interesting. And of course, to give your home a personality—to make it feel lived-in."

"*Lived*-in? It feels *haunted*. And I'm not engaged, I'm frustrated."

"For which I am profoundly sorry, sir. Were your Household Things better trained, you would never have noticed us at all."

"I find that hard to believe."

"You never noticed us before."

"Wait a minute. Are you responsible for carting our cookware all over the house?"

"You see—that's exactly what I mean. That unfortunate incident was perpetrated by the Thing That Misplaces Your Belongings—a Household Thing unversed in the Protocols. No Thing under my tutelage would have made such a gross error as to move that box to the target area so quickly."

"Target area? Protocols? What are you talking about?"

"Domestic Protocols, sir. You can't run a household without them. Take, for example, your cookware. Protocol requires that the movement of such articles be made in logical increments over time so that if the movement is noticed it can be easily attributed to the natural propensity of people to displace items that are in the way. So your cookware should have been moved from the kitchen floor to the top of the refrigerator, or to the floor of an adjacent room. Then it should have been moved to sit among those boxes that are still halfway up your staircase."

Harry detected a note of reproach in that "still." "We've been busy."

"Of course you have, sir. And so, unfortunately, have your Household Things. They saw fit to take your cookware directly from the kitchen floor, under the table, to the upstairs bathroom atop the étagère."

"The what?"

"The shelved unit above the toilet tank."

"Why there?"

Jeeves shrugged as if that should be the most obvious thing in the world. "A simple case of geometry. Each house is divided into quadrants. Likewise each room. Articles are moved so as to end up in the quadrant opposite the one in which they were originally located. So, from the lowest point along the southwest wall of your kitchen..."

"To the highest point on the northeast wall of our upstairs bathroom."

"Precisely, sir. You have a keen grasp of the situation."

"Thanks. So, everything we own is going to be moved around like this forever?"

"Oh no, sir. Every object has a particular place in which it belongs. We move only objects that are not where they belong. The cookware was on the floor under your kitchen table. Not at all where it belonged, sir."

"Uh-huh. Does everybody have...Things?"

"Every man, woman, and child who inhabits a domicile built or remodeled since 1900."

"Siberian sheepherders?"

"They call them *domovoi*, sir. Siberia is not the backwater you might think it is. Now, sir, I really must go. I've broken Protocol in discussing this with you, but

I felt an apology was imperative." He executed a smart little bow and said, "Good-day, sir. I promise we will do better."

Harry reached out to prevent him from leaving, but the front door banged open, startling him.

"Da-ad!" Kim's voice carried up the stairs. "I brought some friends home. We're going to the den to study."

Harry took his eyes off the Head Thing for only a second, but it was enough. He was gone.

"Hey!" Harry stage whispered. Then louder: "*Hey*! Where'd you go?"

"The *den*, Dad. Why?"

Harry crossed the hall to look down the stairs. Kim had poked her head back into the foyer and was peering up at him.

"It's nothing. Just...have fun."

"Yeah. Right. Fun." She disappeared.

Harry made a systematic search of the second floor, but found nothing. He spent the remainder of the day in a state between credulity and denial. He considered telling Marilyn, but she'd only say he was over-stressed. Was he? Undoubtedly. But he'd never heard of stress manifesting itself as a six-foot-seven "Jeeves" archetype who claimed he'd been working for you unseen for umpteen years. No, he couldn't tell Marilyn.

In the end, he decided there was only one person in the family who wouldn't think he was nuts if he started asking questions about Things That Go Bump in the Night, and she was at the mall.

To kill time, he ran experiments. He collected odd items—useless keys, a penlight, one of Meg's bevy of Furbees—and put them in places they definitely did not belong. Then he went into the kitchen and unpacked the remainder of the boxes there. When he went back to check on his experiments he met with uneven results. The keys and Furbee were gone, the penlight was right where he'd left it.

He embarked on a systematic search of the premises based on what Jeeves (possibly a figment of his imagination) had told him about protocols. He'd left the Furbee on the hearth in the living room; he looked for it on the bookshelf on the opposite side of the room. No luck. He moved to the foyer next. Nothing.

Okay. Cut to the chase. If our Things are extremists, then the Furbee should be... He sprinted upstairs to Meg's room—opposite side of the house, second floor, opposite quadrant.

The Furbee was sitting atop the window casement in Meg's room.

Next, he looked for the keys. He'd left them under the sink in the kitchen. He found them, as insanely expected, atop the étagère in the upstairs bathroom.

What did that mean? That there really were Things living in his house that misplaced toys, lurked in closets, and returned empty cartons of milk to the fridge? Or that he was coming unglued?

Marilyn arrived home with Megan at last, sporting Macy's bags. They marched through the front door and up the stairs, brushing past Harry where he hovered on the landing.

"Hi, hon." Marilyn airmailed him a kiss. "Meg, sweetie, I'm going to go put my things away, then I'll help you with yours."

"I'll help her," Harry volunteered.

Marilyn stopped and stared. "You? Mr. Wad-it-up-and-throw-it-in-the-nearest-drawer?"

"I don't—" Harry began and stopped. *He* didn't. But apparently Some*thing* did. "I'll be careful."

"Uh-huh. I'll inspect the results."

Marilyn sailed into the master suite with a rustling

of bags. Harry, meanwhile, ushered Meg into her room and emptied the contents of her bag onto her bed.

"Look at this pretty dress Mommy got me," she enthused, holding up the article.

"Oooh," said Harry. "Let's hang it up." He snagged the dress and opened the closet.

"Mommy cuts the tags off, first," Megan said.

"Oh. Well, you can do that the first time you wear it, okay?"

She shrugged.

Harry made a big deal out of finding a hanger, pushing aside clothes to peer into the closet's dark corners. Nothing.

"Say, Meggie…about the guy who hides in your closet."

"Uh-huh." She was standing next to him holding another dress.

"Is he there all the time?"

"No. Only at night."

"You've seen him?"

"Uh-huh." She handed him the dress.

"What does he look like?"

"He looks like that guy in the funny Frankenstein movie. The one with the buggy eyes."

"He looks like Marty Feldman?"

She shrugged and went back to the bed for another outfit. "But he wears a black super-hero suit."

"When did you see the funny Frankenstein movie?"

"Only a little of it. Then I sneezed and Mom made me go back to bed."

"So you don't mind this guy being in your closet?"

"Uh-uh. He finds lost stuff. Besides, I'm kinda scared of the dark sometimes, so I'm glad he's there. But I don't like it when he hides under my bed. He snores. The other guy didn't snore. And I'm afraid if he stays there, the other guy won't come back."

Harry sat weakly on the foot of the bed. "The *other* guy?"

"Yeah. The one who's *s'posed* to hide under my bed."

"And what does *he* look like?"

She shrugged. "I dunno. I've never seen him. But he bumps so I know he's there. But he doesn't *snore*."

"How long have you known about these...guys?"

"Well, before we moved, I *thought* they were there, but I wasn't sure. I thought they might be piglets of my imagination."

"Figments, honey," Harry corrected absently.

"Oh. Anyway, I wasn't *sure* they were there until we moved into this house. That's when I *saw* them. I think they're elves."

Elves. "Are...are you sure?"

She gave him a wounded look. "Daddy, I *saw* them. I wouldn't make something like that up."

No, Harry thought, she probably wouldn't.

Lying in bed that night, he went over it drowsily for the zillionth time: the Thing lurking behind the bathroom door, the Things in Meg's room, the experiments that seemed to prove Jeeves's Domestic Protocols.

Suddenly wide awake, Harry found his head galloping with wild thoughts. He rolled out of bed, pulled on a T-shirt and a pair of sweatpants, then hesitated. How do you contact someone who wants to remain hidden? Someone who may very well be, as Meg put it, a piglet of your imagination?

He tiptoed into Meg's room and poked his head into the closet. "Hey," he whispered. "You. Thing That Hides in the Closet—I need to talk to your boss."

The closet was silent. Meg mumbled in her sleep.

"Please. I really need to talk to the—the Chief Thingie, or whatever you call him."

Still nothing. But the feeling of being watched sent serious willies up his spine.

"C'mon, guy. I'm not kidding. This is important!"

"Sir?"

Harry stifled a yelp and spun around. Jeeves stood behind him, his basset eyes glistening in the light from the hall. Harry hurried him out of Meg's room.

"All that stuff about protocols and procedures— that applies to *all* Things *everywhere*?"

"Well, of course, sir. Without Protocols, you have chaos."

"And the protocols are always the same?"

"Naturally, sir."

"Okay. You implied that our Household Things are rookies because they came with a new house."

He nodded solemnly.

"What about a house that's just been through a major remodel, new appliances, furniture, window treatments, the works? Would that have a rookie crew?"

"Indubitably."

Harry clapped a hand on the tall guy's shoulder. "Jeeves—may I call you 'Jeeves'?—you've been immensely helpful. Thanks."

"Jeeves is fine, sir." He smiled in a way that reminded Harry of the Eeyore puppet perched on Megan's bedpost. "Is there anything else?"

"Yeah. Are you guys some kind of…elves?"

Jeeves looked positively morose. "We've been called that, sir. But we are Things. Nothing more; nothing less."

"Great. Thanks. I'm going back to bed now. Have a nice night, Jeeves."

"Thank you, sir. And you."

"We've been over this, counselor," said Detective Price. "If Combs had a gun, he didn't hide it here."

"I think he did. Just not where we expected." Harry stood in the entry of Ernest Combs's cottage, flanked by Detectives Price and Kirwan. "You thought he'd hidden it in the broiler pan, right?"

"Right," said Kirwan. "But he hadn't."

Harry glanced through the kitchen portal to the Viking range, then made a beeline for the stairs.

"Where are you going?" Kirwan asked.

Harry didn't answer. He wanted to say something nonchalant and cocky, something James Bond might have said, but as he might be about to make a fool of himself, he stifled the urge.

On the upstairs landing, he turned and scanned the attic bedroom's left-hand wall. It was dominated by the woodstove. Heart pounding, mouth dry, Harry moved to the stove, aware of the eyes on his back. He looked up, following the stovepipe. About six feet off the floor a handle stuck out of the pipe. It looked like a tapered spring with a porcelain knob at one end. Above it, a metal cuff encircled the pipe.

"What's that?" Harry pointed at the handle.

"Flue handle," said Price. "You turn it to adjust the flow of air."

Harry turned the handle. Something rattled down the stovepipe and dropped heavily into the firebox. He opened the stove door, squatted, and peered in. There, at the bottom of the empty firebox was a handgun. Harry pulled a pen out of his coat pocket, fished the gun out, and held it up for inspection. It was a .38 Smith and Wesson.

Kirwan made a sound like a cat hocking up a fur ball.

"I'll be damned," said Price.

"I don't get it," said Kirwan, watching Harry bag the gun. "How'd you do that?"

Harry shrugged. "Just a hunch."

"Some hunch. There is no way Combs had time to come up here, slide that cuff up, and slip the gun onto the flue."

"Yeah," said Price. "And even at that I'd swear we looked there. C'mon, Harry, how'd you come to think of it, really?"

"Something a...a friend of mine said about what happens when you put things where they don't belong."

"Let me guess," said Kirwan. "A forensics guy?"

Harry waggled his head. "Not exactly. Just someone who knew a Thing or two."

Maya Kaathryn Bohnhoff is addicted to speculative fiction. For this, she blames her dad and Ray Bradbury. Her novels include the New York Times Bestseller, *Star Wars Legends: The Last Jedi*. Her short fiction has appeared in Analog, Amazing Stories, Interzone, and others. She has been a finalist for the Campbell, Crawford, Nebula, Sidewise, and British SF awards. Her most recent novel, *The Antiquities Hunter* (Pegasus), is also her debut crime novel and introduces a new female sleuth to the crime scene: Gina Miyoko, PI. She is a founding member of Book View Cafe. In an alternate existence, Maya writes, performs and records music with husband, Jeff. Visit her website: www.mayabohnhoff.com

About the story

Many of my stories come about because of a chance encounter with a news item, a meme, a billboard, a stray comment, or NPR. In this case I saw a single panel cartoon that proposed to answer the age-old question: Why, when I put two socks into my dryer, does only one sock leave? In the cartoon, a woman tosses socks into her dryer in the back of which is a trapdoor with a tunnel that leads down to a nest of leprechauns.

I pondered this, and the fate of other lost items— wallets, keys, toys—and asked the question that has been on the lips of science fiction and fantasy writers since we "penned" our tales with natural pigments on cave walls: What if?

The result was "The Nature of Things", which is also told in song and which features in a larger story that I am hoping to finish someday, if I can just find my favorite Parker ballpoint pen.

Golden Spider Beetles

Shannon Page

The infestation begins in tragedy, then worsens.

Cecilia stands in front of her house, hands on hips, staring at the edge of the roof. At the nest.

She had been so excited when the birds built their home of sticks and feathers in the eaves. Ryan had wanted to knock it down, but she hadn't let him. "Baby birds! We'll hear them peeping from our bedroom window in the morning."

They had never peeped.

Instead, they had died aborning, or a-hatching. The adults soon abandoned the nest, and perhaps each other. Who knew? They were only birds.

What Cecilia does know, now, standing and staring at the devastation, the terrible disgusting *wrongness* of it, is that the golden spider beetles had come next. In the natural order of things. The fellow from the township who has come to look into the matter, who has introduced himself as Duncan—simply Duncan, no last name, or maybe that is his last name?—is explaining it to her quite carefully. With a disturbing intensity, in fact.

According to Duncan, the spider beetles lay eggs

in the fresh corpses of baby birds. The beetle larvae feed on decaying birdflesh. When they are mature, the beetles go off to cause more trouble.

"Why did they die?"

"Die?" He stares at her. She can almost hear him thinking: *The beetles are quite alive*.

"The birds, the baby birds. Why?"

The man shrugs. "Things die."

"They won't damage the house? The bugs?" Cecilia looks at Duncan, trim and tidy in a somewhat shiny blue suit, well-worn leather satchel at his side. The very picture of efficiency and order: reassuring, she supposes.

Too bad he has to destroy the whole effect with his odd manner. His buggy eyes and thin, insectile arms.

"No, they don't eat the wood, do they." Cecilia lets out her breath, but Duncan goes on. "They'll make their way inside, though, and that, you don't want that."

She is already shaking her head. No, she doesn't want that. "Why not?"

His eyes bulge as he stares at her. She has a creeping sense that he is stifling laughter, though his face remains placid. "Your clothes. They'll burrow in your clothes, specially the oily ones. And your kitchen—the beans, the rice, wheat—what have you. They might likely start a whole new nest there, they will. And then where will you be?"

Cecilia shivers with disgust. Does he find this amusing? It must take a special sort of person to become a—whatever he was. The man who gets sent around when something unpleasant needs dealing with. Like an undertaker, or those people the constables hire to tidy up crime scenes after the evidence has been carted off, only the excess blood and bodily waste left behind. And all this knowledge of insects. *Golden spider beetles*, for crying out loud. What kind of person wanted to learn the intricate details of bugs, and then kill them?

Then one of his phrases worms its way back into her slow-moving thoughts. Oily clothes? Is this just more of the pervasive, subtle nastiness the English have shown her ever since she and Ryan came to live here, eleven long months ago?

"No," she says, and takes a step away from the weird little man. "We have to get rid of them. Do it— whatever you need to do." She is nearly at the road before she remembers yet again that she has looked the wrong way for traffic. Did one ever get used to this?

Stopping on the kerb, she turns and looks right, but no cars are coming, and she isn't actually going any- where. Just…getting away from the horror. A few steps.

"First thing we have to do is take that nest down."

Cecilia nods. She cannot watch.

"Yes. Do it."

In bed, in their bed: this is where home is, where love happens. She pulls Ryan close, holds him against her breast, wends her fingers through his soft hair. In this moment, she can pretend she owns him.

He does always return to her. After all, he has followed Cecilia here in the first place, when her uncle died and left her this house, under the peculiar, even eccentric, condition that she inhabit it for one year, without leaving.

Crazy Uncle Horace, she even called him, always with a laugh. He made such a great story, her mother's (yes) eccentric brother, living all alone in England in his weird old house. Studying bugs, of all things.

Horace would have known what to do about the golden spider beetles.

She hadn't needed to accept the inheritance; Ryan had a perfectly decent house in Boston, as he had pointed out to her patiently, more than once. More than ten times, if she were honest. But she took it, she signed the papers in the lawyer's office, she agreed to the terms. It would be something of her own.

Had she been running away from Ryan? Was he supposed to have followed?

And what did 'leaving' mean, exactly? About the house, and her duty to it. The codicil had not specified. She has been staying close to home these eleven months, just to be safe. A few trips to town. Plenty of work in the yard. Lots and lots of cooking.

Never spending a night away. Not for any reason.

Now, in their bed, Cecilia digs a garden-ragged fingernail into Ryan's scalp, twining his lush hair and giving it a yank. He moans, pleasure and pain tied up in one long sweet exhalation, his breath shockingly cool against her sweat-slick skin. This. This is what they can do.

She sighs and tilts her head back, her mind rippling through the sensations in her body, her eyes nearly unseeing. She almost doesn't catch the small movement above the dark drapes, where wall meets ceiling.

In the kitchen, she takes stock. Literally and figuratively: she has boiled the roots and parings and bones and leftovers all week to make a soup base, and it will soon be a magnificent thing. Such a thin and weedy soup stock they make here; nothing like what her mother taught her, back across the wild blue sea. She can show these English folk a thing or two.

More to the point is the figurative stock-taking: here she is. A house, a yard, a half-mile of narrow stony road, a strip of garden, a country village.

An infestation.

Duncan from the township has been and gone three times already; by the end, Cecilia had been entertaining bizarre thoughts. Of him coming up behind her, cupping hands beneath her breasts, running fingers over the buttons of her blouse, reaching down to unzip her jeans... But the buggy, bulgy eyes kept interrupting even this bit of imaginary adventure, and ultimately she paid him and sent him off. By check— or, cheque, as they would have it here. Extra letters in everything. Favour, aluminium, catalogue, rumour.

Pleasoure? No, of course not.

⸻◆⸻

Things That May or May Not Be Food, Depending Upon Your Culture, Your Upbringing, Your Frame of Mind, or Your General State of Starvation and/or Addiction:

Marrow

Fermented grapes

Larvae

Cats

Crustaceans

Fungi

Grasshoppers

Dried leaves in boiling water

Ostrich

Beetles

"What are you doing?"

Startled, Cecilia looks up. Ryan stands in the doorway of the study. It is late afternoon; painterly light slants down across the surface of Horace's writing desk.

No, *her* writing desk. Hers now.

"I—" she starts, and then realizes she doesn't know. She looks down at the piece of thick creamy stationery, the heavy fountain pen in her right hand.

The peculiar list she has clearly written.

"Nothing." She pushes the paper to the back of the desk, covers it with an invoice from the town council as she rises and faces her husband.

———◆———

Ryan sips his sherry and smiles at Cecilia. His eyes glitter, reflecting the candlelight. "The soup is lovely, thank you."

She nods, pleased, and maybe a little proud. "You're welcome."

He sits forward, something important on his lips. She can almost feel the words before he says them. "I have to go up to London tomorrow. I shan't be back before the weekend, I don't imagine."

Shan't. Now he's talking like them. He mimics the accent too, this low, lilting song that is the English way of speaking, dropping at the end of the sentence.

It is not important. She probably does it as well. It's almost irresistible.

I shan't ever stop being American, she tells herself. *I shan't I shan't I shan't.*

Ryan is waiting for her to say something, she realizes. "All right." She smiles at him across the table, the lace tablecloth, the rich and hearty soup. "That's fine."

"Come with me. We'll go to the theatre, we'll eat out. You used to like to come when I traveled."

"You know I can't."

"Going to London for a few days is not *leaving*. Honestly! It's nearly a year already anyway."

"Not quite. Why be stupid? I'd lose the house."

He's still smiling, he's holding that smile so hard. She can see him try to find soft words. She knows the words he wants to say are...not soft. "I just don't see..." He doesn't finish the sentence.

"I'll be fine here." And now she smiles at him. The urge to reassure is deeply ingrained. "I'll go with you next month."

"Of course." He brightens. "I'll talk to the Gibsons. They can send that man round to look in on you."

Duncan. "No." She shakes her head, smiling, frowning, fighting down—what? Not panic, not fear, just...something. "No need, I'm perfectly safe here. You're away overnight plenty." Did he hear the complaint?

Did he hear the relief under the complaint?

Ryan reaches over and pats her hand. It is the one holding the soup spoon. A bit of the thick broth spills onto the tablecloth. He does not notice. "This is *four* nights, Cecilia. I insist."

She pushes his hand away and gets up to clear the bowls. Out of the corner of her eye, she sees something drop to the table. It lands there, shiny-bright against the tablecloth. It is a golden spider beetle, glittering and lovely, in the spot of soup.

Cecilia hears her own gasp as though through a cloud of gauze, or a river, or a dream.

In a dream, time is bent and wrapped and shoved and pushed over.

In a dream, glowing sharp fractals merge and moisten and invade.

In a dream, a butterfly wing glistens on your skin and you shiver with the force of it.

In a dream, beetles shimmer.

———◆———

She awakens in bed, though she knows she did not put herself there. Her clothes are still on, for one thing, though her shirt has been untucked, and hairpins are scattered over the marble-topped bedside table. Probably not all of them, but enough to ease her scalp, to let her tangled tresses flow about her shoulders, and make her all hot and uncomfortable.

Why is it so warm? And dark. The light is somehow wrong—it is daytime, but the sun is missing.

Cecilia murmurs, an indistinct sound even to her own ears. What is she trying to say? She is calling out for help, for comfort…she is not calling for Ryan.

Ryan is many things but comfort is not one of them.

The man Duncan is there, perched beside the bed like a praying mantis, his bony little hands folded before him. Moving slowly against one another with a quiet scritch of dry skin on skin. "Mam?" he whispers.

Why is this man in her bedroom?

"Get out." She tries to make her voice cold and unfeeling, but knows that she has only managed whiny. If she could only mimic the accent…

Duncan nods, but does not rise. Has he even understood her?

"Get *out*," she says, more forcefully.

"Mam, your husband insisted I sit with you until you can tend to yourself," he says, still nodding in that foolish way.

Ryan. Why wasn't he here? Damn him, did he go to London? How long has she been…? She glances over at the window, away from Duncan.

And then looks again.

"What happened to the wall?"

Duncan follows her gaze, taking in the planking and boards. It's a hastily hammered-up mess of scraps and siding and what looks like a sheet of fabric. Her curtains are nowhere to be seen; neither is the window.

"The beetles, Mam; I told you about the beetles. They got in the walls, they did. We got them out, but now the walls are rotten."

"You said they didn't destroy wood. You said clothes, food..." Cecilia sits up and rubs her eyes, trying to make sense of it, trying to remember. *What* day *is it?* Duncan averts his eyes; she pulls the covers up over her loosened shirt. Stupid, it is; he's obviously been sitting here long enough to see whatever he might like.

What is it about men that they always feel they must pretend? A woman would see what she saw and make no nonsense about it. A man—he would blink, and dissemble, and hem and haw and clear his throat, just as this thin and nervous creature is doing.

Cecilia opens her mouth to say—something, to ask for a drink of water or complain about the heat or send him downstairs for food—but then she sees what he is looking at. The golden spider beetles have not been removed at all. They pour around the edges of the blacked-out window, teeming down the walls, their arid legs rasping against each other, hundreds of them, thousands of them, making their way toward her...

She cringes in the bed, drawing away from the horrid little man, even as he reaches for her, his mouth a rictus grin, a beetle grasped in his pale white hand...

———◆———

Darkness comes.

Darkness, easing along the edges, seeping through to the center.

Darkness, inky black, raw and rough and unrefined.

Darkness, a black cat at midnight, with glowering yellow eyes.

Darkness, rose thorns dug into the flesh of your middle finger when you empty the vase and the blood that comes is black and thick and slow and runs down the sink and the counter and onto the marble floor, dripping, dripping, dripping...

"Darling," Ryan says. "Wake up, love."

Cecilia blinks again, but cannot see.

Then she does, and the room is unfamiliar. "Where am I?"

He looks away, and she follows his gaze, confused. Then it falls into place: he has taken her to the infirmary in town. A place she has visited only once, to fill a prescription for some ointment.

"You weren't making any sense," Ryan says, turning back to her with an apologetic smile. "Duncan was frightened, he sent for me. I canceled my meetings and came back, love." He puts his hand on her cheek; it feels cool against her skin.

"Thank you," she says. He came back early. He canceled his meetings. He loves her. It must be so. She was wrong to doubt him...

"I'm taking you back to Boston on the redeye tonight—I've already called Dr. Wongsawat at Beth Israel Deaconess, she's expecting us."

Impossible. Cecilia cringes, pulling away from his hand. He will lose her the house. It will pass to the next heir, a distant cousin in rural France, someone she's never met.

He will own her again.

She was wrong to *not* doubt him, even for a moment there.

A man enters the room. Dr. Gibson: town doctor, leader of the council, and owner of the only pub—in a small village like this, everyone wears many hats. "How are we feeling?" he asks Cecilia, after a meaningful glance at her husband.

She draws herself up, suddenly seeing it all. "No." She scrabbles out of the bed, reaches for a housecoat draped over a chair. "No, this is not right. You can't take me. I can't leave. It's *mine*."

Ryan is on his feet, reaching for her, but the bed blocks him. "Darling...?" His voice is pained, but she's seen that glance, she knows. "You're not well, you lie back down."

"I am fine! You can't take me!"

"It's not worth it!" His anguished tone belies him. "The house is infested, it's worthless! Probably your mad uncle's *pet* bugs! Cecilia, you just need to—"

But she is on the move. Dr. Gibson and Ryan both try to stop her, getting briefly tangled against one another's clumsy movements—the critical moment she needs. Still thrusting her arms through the sleeves of the robe, she bursts out of the room and runs down a stupidly long corridor to the front door.

On the road, she nearly collides with Duncan. He is thinner than ever, his eyes bulging and shining, reflecting the bright sunlight. He holds a large copper-colored key, tied round at its head with a red string.

Her key.

"Mam!" he croaks, stepping back as he attempts to tuck the key into the inside pocket of his shiny blue suit, long, bony fingers poking at the draping folds of fabric, trying to find purchase.

Cecilia snatches the key from his hand and runs down the road toward her home.

"Darling!" Ryan's voice, behind her. He will be too slow, it won't matter. He still doesn't believe she's gone, that he has lost control. "My love!"

She runs out of the tiny town, leaving the infirmary and the pub and the fishmonger and the potter behind. Soon she is in the open air, surrounded by fields, sheep. She takes a deep breath and shouts to the world: a cry of triumph, of freedom, of defiance, without words.

When she turns the last corner and sees the house, she knows she can win. All she has to do is get inside. She can bar the door, be alone forever.

In Horace's house. *Her* house. Safe. Alone. Complete.

Cecilia takes the front steps two at a time, then scrabbles the key in the door, flinging it open. The house admits her. There is a strong odor of sweet decay in the air, something vegetal, heavy. She pushes forward. Her house does not frighten her.

It's what's outside that does that.

She darts into the entry hall, leaning on the door to hold it closed, willing her strength into the old lock. Shouts and footsteps waft up from the road below; then there is knocking on the door, more yelling, even pounding. But the lock holds.

Cecilia ignores the cries. Eventually, they fade. She stands tall, steps away from the door, shaking her hair loose from its tangled knot. A ray of sunlight pierces the transom and glints down to the floor. She breathes deep.

She takes stock.

Why has she not seen it before? The people are distractions. The doctor; the unwelcoming townsfolk; Duncan, the head bug himself.

And Ryan. Pretender to love.

Cecilia steps further into her house, hearing the skittering of tiny feet all around her. She holds herself firm against the onslaught. Embryonic wings unfold; sharp mandibles click.

A beetle falls from the ceiling and lands on her arm. Cecilia jumps, but it's just old habit. They can't hurt her now. In fact they never could.

They feed on death. She is alive.

Cecilia flicks the beetle from her arm and stamps a solid foot on it, mashing it into the hardwood floor.

There is the sound of a chuckle. "*I knew I made the right choice.*"

She turns and faces the spectre of her uncle Horace. He inhabits the corner just to the side of the staircase, glinting like a beetle wing. "Baby birds would have been cuter," she tells him, her voice even. Calm.

He just shrugs and smiles.

"But I guess I can live with beetles."

Then she goes to her kitchen to put on the kettle for tea.

———◆———

Shannon Page was born on Halloween night and spent her early years on a back-to-the-land commune in northern California. A childhood without television gave her a great love of the written word. At seven, she wrote her first book, an illustrated adventure starring her cat Cleo. Sadly, that story is out of print, but her work has appeared in *Clarkesworld*, *Interzone, Fantasy*, *Black Static*, Tor.com, the Proceedings of the 2002 International Oral History Association Congress, and many anthologies, including the Australian Shadows Award-winning *Grants Pass,* and *The Mammoth Book of Dieselpunk.*

Books include contemporary fantasies *The Queen and The Tower* and *A Sword in The Sun,* the first two books in The Nightcraft Quartet; hippie horror novel *Eel River*, story collection *Eastlick and Other Stories;* personal essay collection *I Was a Trophy Wife*; *Orcas Intrigue, Orcas Intruder,* and *Orcas Investigation,* the first three books in the cozy mystery series The Chameleon Chronicles, in collaboration with Karen G. Berry under the pen name Laura Gayle; and *Our Lady of the Islands*, co-written with the late Jay Lake. *Our Lady* received starred reviews from *Publishers Weekly* and *Library Journal*, was named one of *Publishers Weekly*'s Best Books of 2014, and was a finalist for the Endeavour Award. Forthcoming books include Nightcraft books three and four; a sequel to *Our Lady*; and more Orcas mysteries. Edited books include the anthologies *Witches, Stitches & Bitches* and *Black-Eyed Peas on New Year's Day: An Anthology of Hope*, and the essay collection *The Usual Path to Publication.*

Shannon is a longtime yoga practitioner, has no tattoos (but she did recently get a television), and lives on lovely, remote Orcas Island, Washington, with her husband, author and illustrator Mark Ferrari. Visit her at www.shannonpage.net.

About the story

I started with the title. *Of course*. Golden spider beetles! Yes, they really are a thing; yes, they really do have the sort of unsavory habits that the unsavory Duncan tells Cecilia about. And they're really quite pretty: they do look made of gold.

The story practically wrote itself!

Or so I thought.

I wrote the draft ten or more years ago, when I was processing some anger and sorrow from a romantic disappointment. Very therapeutic, of course, to write that stuff out; sadly, not always conducive to a workable story. Okay, the story was terrible. Overwritten, overwrought, overheated—and it didn't really have an ending. Just Cecilia screaming something about *Neither love nor golden spider beetles...*

So I put the story down and moved on. But I always felt like there was *something* there. And then, a decade or more later, when Marissa mentioned she wanted help editing a ghost story anthology, and maybe we should put stories of our own into it too, I finally realized, *Oh.* "Golden Spider Beetles" is a *ghost* story! A few tweaks, some deletions of the worst of the histrionics, an actual conclusion, and there it is.

Borrowed Places

K.E. Kimbriel

"**R**ik, are you—"

That was all Erika caught before her earbuds fell out and slapped her shoulders in passing. There wasn't much she could do about it—Rik was sprinting out the back entrance and off the hill country farmhouse's deck. Spectral energy seethed like an invisible cloud around her, spiking her adrenaline. Her heart was trying to tap dance out of her chest.

A stabbing headache from mold spores inside the house and her skin on fire from the lingering chlorine odor wasn't helping, either.

WHERE WHERE WHERE shrieked the energy battering her mind.

Whatever it was, it was *upset*.

"I can't talk right now, Kam, I'll text you!" Rik gasped, smacking into her faithful (and allergen-free) ancient Toyota Camry. As terror receded, she drew in a deep breath, disconnected the phone, clutched her clipboard to her chest, and turned around. The owner of the recently renovated 120-year-old farmhouse had wandered back outside and was standing on the wood deck.

Mr. Emmons wore a huge grin. "You must be one of the people who can feel it, eh? What do you think, Ms. Rowan? Can we advertise as haunted?"

It took her a moment to sort what she had felt. First, she had to repeat a version of the standard speech. "Mr. Emmons, I'm a property assessor for Borrowed Places, Inc. We are a specialty short-term rental group catering to people with off-the-scale allergy problems like mold, volatile organic compounds—VOCs—from off-gassing plastics, fragrances, cleaners, regional air quality, smoke, and so on. BPI has a Growing Green Star rating for clean places that are environmentally safe in those areas. People with severe allergies will pay a premium for those assurances. Such clients also often have…energy problems." Rik considered the past five minutes and her throbbing head. "They may have trouble with electromagnetic frequencies. They may notice very high or very deep sounds from mechanical equipment in the house. Or…they may notice spectral presences…" She let her words trickle off. "We have a Spectral Orange Star rating for safe energy and friendly or nonthreatening spectral activity."

"Ghosts," Mr. Emmons interrupted.

"You have mold in your basement, Mr. Emmons," she finally got out. "Also, you can't use things like liquid chlorine or commercial cleaners and get a Growing Green Star rating. But it's a beautiful renovation, and I can give you a sheet of what needs to be worked on."

"My wife is a clean freak," he said, the smile sliding off his face. "Dolly never wants anyone to feel like the place is unclean."

Rik took a couple of steps back toward the deck and stopped.

An invisible hand was held up in warning, a cold spectral breeze brushing her face. "And we appreciate her zeal. But some people have problems with VOCs, including artificial fragrances. She needs to investigate some of the organic cleaners, or use unscented ones. Absolutely no plug-ins allowed, and no 'treatments' on that granite countertop."

"How about the ghost?"

Rik allowed a long pause. "What makes you think there's a ghost?"

"Well, something keeps unlocking the deadbolt on the back door. Something opens it when we've locked up, and won't let people unlock it sometimes." Now Mr. Emmons was frowning. "I changed the lock; I have done everything short of rip the door out and start over. Do I need to turn this into a picture window and move the door?"

"Maybe. Do you know anything about the history of your house?" Rik wasn't certain he had an actual ghost—it was the most chaotic energy she had ever run into. "Previous owners, any stories about who lived here? Does it figure in any local history?"

"One family owned it the entire time. The folks that built the original cabin, they hewed those big oak logs almost two hundred years ago for an earlier home, and then hauled them here. We turned that cabin into the living room," he added. "We bought the place from the tax office. Old Mrs. Boone hadn't paid the last year's taxes. She lived a good long life, but she outlived all her kids. Her great-grandkids even left her ashes in boxes out back, in the shed—hers and her youngest son." Emmons shrugged, uncomfortable, as he stepped off the low platform. "Her youngest son was a nice guy, but he never got older than eight or nine, in his head. I can show you the picture he drew of his ma, the last year of his life. The family left that drawing under the ash boxes. And no, I don't know why they didn't bury the ashes."

"I would love to see that picture later, Mr. Emmons. It's hard to give you any input on whether you can advertise as…atmospheric…unless we take care of the mold. It can give people headaches—" Oh, boy, could it "—it can cause some people to feel like they are being watched, can cause anxiety, shortness of breath—" Immune-compromised people can even catch molds, she didn't say, knowing she had caught one at a hundred-plus-year-old hotel.

Mr. Emmons shook his head. "We don't want anyone getting ill while thinking they had a ghost experience. But I'm not looking forward to dealing with mold." He looked off in the distance. "Can you tell where the mold is?"

"I have a pretty good track record at narrowing down the location," Rik replied, carefully scribbling *Grief-stricken ghost?* on her clipboard.

"Well, show me where the mold is, and I'll talk to the missus about it." He nodded once, briskly.

Rik tossed her clipboard into the passenger seat and grabbed her half-respirator mask. "Let's go look." She'd look if she could negotiate entry.

Rik paused at the two steps up to the deck and waited, letting her own internal walls soften slightly. But she felt nothing. *I don't know who or what you are looking for,* Rik thought at the energy.

There was no answer.

I'm OK, Rik texted. *Will explain at dinner.* She tucked her phone back into her small hip pouch.

When she had re-entered the Emmons house to inspect for mold, whatever had chased her out the first time had not tried to drive her off again. In the meantime, Rik had fourteen more inspections on her list. This was the part of her work that her regional supervisor valued the most. Fully sixty percent of the rental properties in the city seemed to have mold. That was Rik's private estimate. Six out of ten, every time she had looked for a new place to live due to sky-rocketing rents. The percentages were like clock-work.

Borrowed Places had found a niche market, and her regional supervisor was thrilled to have not just one but three employees who could sniff out mold or chemical problems. That all three of them were also sensitive to psychic phenomena? That was a bonus.

Just saying that your Bed and Breakfast house was a non-smoking establishment was no longer enough. People's sensitivities had gotten too strong. And those sensitive people would pay twenty-five to fifty percent over most rental prices for guarantees of a clean place to sleep.

Of course people would also pay a great deal more to at least spend the night—if not actually sleep—in a haunted house. The cute little bungalow before her might be an excellent addition to the BPI stable.

But it could be added only if BPI and the owner could strike an agreement with the resident spirit.

"I'm sorry, Miss González," Rik said, handing the young woman a card and a site owner's brochure. "But you cannot get a GGS, a Growing Green Star rating, when you can't enforce your *No Smoking* rule."

Miss González, who looked barely more than a girl, fought to keep her face from crumpling. "But I have scrubbed the walls, even! I don't want to put a camera in the main room of this house, but how else can I keep people honest about it?"

The paper recycling sack resting behind them on the stoop fell over, spilling beer cans. *You could stop renting to students who are easily influenced by a ghost who likes to party.*

"You charge for smoking in the room?" Rik said aloud.

"Two hundred and fifty dollars!"

Rik grimaced. "I know that tends to be the going price, but to clean to our standards, we recommend a threat of a thousand dollars, reserve it on the card, and state that in your rental agreement. Or, require they buy an insurance policy that includes cleaning for smoke— we have two places we recommend for cleaning insurance. You may never get a violation again if you do that—and don't worry about not having renters. People who can be made ill by smoke will gladly pay the premium. Some hosts even scrub chimneys and block fireplace openings."

"I can't stand the chemicals those companies use to clean smoke out of the carpet and couch," the woman admitted, winding a finger in a long curl. "I don't know what else to do."

Rik gestured to get her to walk away from the stoop, so that her party-hound ghost might not overhear what Rik had to say next. "Well, some people have luck cleaning bad odors and smoke particulates with an ozone generator," she said. "We do not recommend them—go read up at the EPA about them—because you should not leave them for renters to use, or run them while people are in the rental property. Ozone is not safe to breathe. But the generators, in my experience, are excellent in neutralizing odors in soft materials and the air. You could invest in one, and you will always be prepared to clear the air if someone does this again. Also? Get an indoor air quality monitor. It will give you proof of violations without an intrusive camera."

"I've tried not renting on game weekends, but those are the big money-makers!" González tried to control her anxiety, but her eyebrows twitched.

Rik gave the house a long look. "Previous owner liked to party?"

Now it was Miss González's turn for a long look. "What have you heard?"

"Let's say, there is something lingering here that really misses tailgating," Rik murmured.

The young woman shrieked, but she didn't seem horrified. "I knew it! I knew it! It is haunted, isn't it?" She did a little dance in a circle. "Can we advertise it?"

"If we can figure out how to let the ghost enjoy a quiet party without smoke or fragrances, maybe you can."

Rik rested her weight on her left leg, looking hard at the snug stone and oak bungalow. She saw nothing with her eyes, but someone seemed to lean against her shoulder, murmuring "Frat guy" in her ear. She could almost see the young ghost...almost.

It was as if the house looked back, a cigar in one hand and a can of beer in the other.

Rik looked at the owner. "You have a great little property, Miss González. I know you would like the GGS rating, but we also have a 'reputed to be haunted—guests must sign a spectral waiver' rating. You can't charge quite as much rent for that as for a GGS, but a Spectral Orange Star rating and an ozone generator might be the way to go with this house."

"Could we convince a ghost to stop egging on the party-hearty guests?" Now the owner was also looking back at the house.

They watched two cans roll out of the paper sack and trace a curve on the sidewalk at the base of the stairs. The González woman sucked in air through her teeth.

"Owners can sometimes negotiate a truce with a spirit," Rik said slowly. "I haven't seen anyone successfully do it with a rental property. It's either you put up with the ghost, or you try to exorcise it."

Miss González frowned. "I can't advertise an exorcised ghost."

"No. And exorcism can sometimes go wrong, if it's not the correct ritual for the ghost." Boy, could it go wrong. There was that ghost who tossed full cans of pop at a fleeing ghost hunter. "You don't want an angry ghost. You want a tolerant and maybe occasionally mischievous ghost. A friendly ghost. A helpful ghost. You will rarely be able to rent this place overnight if you have a grumpy ghost."

"I suppose not." González looked just a little disappointed.

"There are people who have grumpy ghosts who make half their year renting at extreme prices for the month of October," Rik said carefully. "They make the rest of their money during the huge music festivals when people are paying twice the monthly mortgage for a place to stay. But if someone panics and runs through a screen door or dives through a window, that can be very, very expensive."

"Let's keep the ghost friendly," the owner said, nodding until her curls bobbed.

Good idea.

<hr>

The next two houses were so bad with mold that Rik strapped on her respirator before she even entered. As she walked around the outsides of the houses, mold spores brushed her skin, triggering a sharp headache of warning.

At the next house Rik could detect no mold when she examined the exterior, so she left her respirator in its container.

She managed two steps inside and suddenly could

not breathe. Her chest tightened. Her lungs locked. *Dammit!*

Apparently, the owner did not like the old-house odor his property had. He had put a different fragrance of plug-in in every room.

Ducking back outside, Rik drew in deep gasps of air for about a minute. *Plug-ins!* She opened her snap-top plastic container and put on her respirator.

This visit wouldn't go well.

Then there was the mid-fifties modern house down-town. Rik arrived early. Some new plumbing work, a new wood floor in the back bedroom—the pictures had looked great, but she needed to check the odor on the new floor and adhesive... Nice kitchen, great picture windows over a wooded section of a public park...

Rik walked around the attached deck to check out the view. Live oak and bigtooth maple trees wove a leafy wall between the house and a softball diamond down the hill. Oh, a green and gold cathedral, this had real potential. Taking a deep breath, she smelled forest, not car fumes. This was even better than she'd hoped. Turning, Rik looked into the bedroom window, at the dark paneling and crisp lines of the original house.

Something looked back at her. Something her eyes could not see.

It didn't want company.

Rik was back in her car with the doors locked before she dared to start thinking again.

What in creation was that? How did she know something was there? But something was there—she'd bet money on it. She took slow, deep breaths, slowing her racing heart, letting her boundaries grow thinner just a bit...

Longing for peace, seeking privacy and tranquility...I will stay here...

Unlike the spirit at the Emmons place, this entity wasn't looking for anyone or anything. It had found what it was looking for: solitude. Rik pulled herself back into the Now. How could she negotiate with a rather private ghost?

She almost jumped out of her skin when someone tapped on her driver's side window. "Borrowed Places?" a low voice said. Grabbing her clipboard and also the container for her respirator in case of VOCs, Rik climbed out of her sedan.

"Hi, I'm Erika Rowan," she said as she got out. "Morgan?" The newcomer nodded. "Let's see if I can negotiate entry," Rik added quietly.

The tall, lanky individual in jeans and a black silk jacket momentarily clasped hands over mouth. Then a whisper slipped out: "I've had two workmen and one renter tell me they felt *watched* here. You mean something is really here?"

"Oh, yeah. It doesn't seem to want visitors who know it's here. That could be a problem." Rik stopped on the front deck. *I don't want to stay.* "It...doesn't like change."

"Poor thing." The owner continued to whisper, as if that would stop a ghost from hearing them. "Life is change. But I had to fix the house up or the city would have condemned it and torn it down."

The sound of popping came from inside the house.

How about quiet guests? Rik sent that thought into the house, trying to communicate with the ghost. *Would you leave the quiet ones alone? Would you tolerate people who only listened to music and...watched TV? No parties?*

The silence didn't feel hostile. The owner opened the heavy front door and walked in. Rik carefully stepped over the threshold.

A complete tour followed. Two bedrooms, two small but stylish baths, a very nice kitchen, no basement, not much storage, good sitting room and deck, several fifties-style furniture pieces, and most importantly, no mold, no harsh chemicals or weird fragrances lingering. "You had them use low VOC adhesive, didn't you?"

Morgan grinned. "Yes, and the floor is real oak, not composite. I got it at Restoration Remainders." Morgan gestured at the room. "It's small enough that I could afford the real wood I wanted. I was hoping Borrowed Places would give me a good rating."

"This is lovely," Rik said quickly. "Are you thinking about using multiple listings, or just switching to BPI?"

"Oh, I wanted your agency, if possible. I thought I could protect the house and the...spirit...better with Borrowed Places." Morgan stumbled only slightly, as if admitting the ghost was real was a new experience.

Rik waited to see if the ghost would somehow comment.

The feeling of watchfulness increased, and she felt a brush of cool air.

"I'd like to live in this house someday," Morgan admitted. "I love the peace of it. I wouldn't mind sharing with a nice quiet...roommate. Plus, if I were to sell the house, the new owner would probably tear it down and build new. And the poor ghost might be stuck with a new house full of noisy college students."

"You're right. Tearing down a haunted house doesn't always mean the ghost leaves—and sometimes the ghost fights back."

"I'm not sure it likes so much coming and going. Does that mean it would hate it if I rent the house out a lot?" Morgan's comment sounded deliberately vague. Rik suspected that Morgan had not discussed ghosts or problems renting with any friends.

Well, people who felt or saw ghosts tended to be careful who they told about those ghosts.

"Do you have to rent it?" Rik asked. "Or could you live here and rent where you are now? Do you own the place where you're living?"

An old gear clock chimed sweetly.

Morgan stared at Rik for a moment. "I inherited this from my great-uncle," they said slowly. "Actually, I do have a second place a few blocks from here. I have a mortgage on it."

"If it's a few blocks from here, you could arrange a GGS rating and rent the other place to tech contractors or tourists," Rik went on. "Have you got a picture of it?"

Wordlessly, Morgan pulled out a phone and made a few passes on the screen. Then they showed Rik an upgraded large bungalow with what looked like heirloom roses to either side of stone steps.

Rik squinted slightly. No gray haze...no mold in the house. "Is the idea worth thinking about tonight? You can tell me tomorrow what you want to do."

"I had never considered..." Morgan closed the photo. "Yeah, it's worth thinking about. I was just rushing to protect this place and cover the property taxes."

"Since you have done rentals before, for this place we could set you up fast for next month with a 'spectral waiver' required and 'quiet revenant unless you are too noisy or try to interact with it' or some such notice—"

The clock chimed again.

"Some people don't like chiming clocks," Rik went on, turning to survey the living room. "I didn't see—"

"No clock."

Rik turned back. Morgan's face was impassive.

"Have you heard that before?"

Morgan gave a very slight nod of affirmation.

"I was just thinking that if your...great-uncle's roommate wouldn't mind a few October renters at twice the going rate, you could knock off half the property tax in four weeks."

They stared at each other.

Rik said aloud, "So you like the idea of longer term, quiet renters, but you don't want to spend years with strangers?" A very faint chime sounded. Rik locked gazes with the owner, who lifted their eyebrows. *And while we are here...* "Do you like the new owner?"

This time the chime was strong.

"Actually," Rik went on, "a chiming clock that isn't there is a fun way to totally freak out people who don't think ghosts exist."

The owner smothered a cough.

"You'd want the spectral waiver so that guests will owe a kill fee, at least fifty percent, if they suddenly are not so excited about staying in a haunted house. Plus, if you get a ghost hunter with equipment, your ghost might mess with them. And the ghost hunter, or the ghost, might make a mess."

Morgan looked around the tranquil living room with a tender longing on their face. "Maybe I will just move in."

Chords of spectral chimes heralded an hour that wasn't there.

"I think your ghost likes you," Rik murmured. "You're on the same wavelength."

That was the best visit—and visitation—all day, even if Borrowed Places didn't get this listing.

Rik met her fellow property assessor Kam for dinner at a new food trailer with grass-fed beef BBQ on the menu.

Kam had raved about the place, so Rik was game.

"You get hurt?" Kam asked bluntly as they met in the parking lot.

It took Rik a moment to remember when she'd been talking with Kam. "Nah, it wasn't mean. It was...frantic," she said slowly. "Yelling 'Where where where' in my head. I think it doesn't know where its people went."

"Damn, those are hard ones. I was way out today, farm BnB types." Without pause Kam rattled off her order to the person at the register, glanced Rik's way and added, "Two, please."

"We're actually making a lot of progress with adding new locations," Rik pointed out as she claimed a table and handed her friend cash for the meal. "I approved three places today. All GGS, quiet locations, one a first-time renter. And three—no, maybe four—great possibles. Three of those SOS with spirit, one an unknown."

"I found one, just one. Also a couple of owners who were snotty about how strong their 'natural' cleaning supplies smelled, and one really active ghost—as in, following-us-around active. I'm not sure it wants so much coming and going as will happen if the place becomes a rental."

"That could be a problem," Rik agreed. She double-checked the table for grease or mold, but it was scrubbed clean. "My last location was pretty active, too."

"Bunch of moldy houses," Kam went on, frowning, her gaze flickering over the people in line. "It's so hard to tell them that you sense 'allergens' in a place without using the 'M' word. People panic. They're afraid you are gonna tell the world."

"Yeah, it's bad enough when we stop at the entry and won't go in," Rik said, nodding. *And of course two of us can tell by looking at a picture.* **Nobody** *wants to know that.*

"So counting yesterday's viewings, we have eight new listings as of today, if all the owners sign? And six of them want to be exclusive?" Kam asked, looking back at Rik.

"Yes. I like the Emmons place as a possible, too. We just have to convince the wife that she doesn't have to sandblast with chlorine and flower scent after every guest, and her husband will have to fix the mold in the basement. And if we could just calm down the spirit energy. It's a distinctive little house."

"So what about the *González* place?" Kam gave her a wide, close-lipped smile.

"Did you go look at that?" Rik gave her a Look.

Kam's grin grew broader. "Drove by. Not sure I should go in. That ghost wants to share a brew with somebody."

Rik smothered a snort of laugher. "Maybe the owner needs to throw a party in the back yard every quarter or something. Otherwise it will have to be a Spectral Orange Star rating only." Rik jumped up at the trailer owner's arm waving in their direction. The place gave trays, so she brought the food back and returned the tray before sitting down.

"A quarterly gathering is not necessarily a bad idea." Kam pulled out her traveling chopsticks and attacked the meat.

"And the mid-century modern—if the owner goes with occasional renting, maybe we can do it as monthly with a quiet revenant rating, or just October and music festivals. But I'm not counting on it," Rik added. "Owner loves that house and really wants to hide there with the ghost. However, they own another place a few blocks away. Maybe they will trade ghost and mid-century for a comfortable bungalow and short-term tech rentals. Might be too much to hope for that they'll go for tech rentals plus October mid-century." Rik paused, and then gave Kam wiggled eyebrows. "The vintage has a ghost clock that chimes."

"Oh, I hate the ghost clocks. They are not regular, and then you are left wondering if it's a comment or a warning."

Rik laughed and tore up her BBQ to toss in her smoked beans.

The next morning Kam headed west into the "big bucks" part of town, as many properties came with carriage houses and granny pods that the owners were looking to rent, while Rik went south into a mixed region of new suburban and vintage homes.

Rain had washed most of the city clean, and the south looked inviting.

It *should* have looked inviting.

Rik drove through a small section several times, noting the alternating houses that had mold, and then didn't have mold. That meant a battle for the mold-free owners, as mold eventually threw off spores, and those spores traveled to nearby houses.

Normally she'd stop first to meet the person who wanted to rent, but *something* in this neighborhood was very off.

The jangling, discordant feeling wasn't coming from 12 Emily D. West Drive, the house she had been sent to inspect. Then where was the trouble?

Rik narrowed it down to 20 Emily D. West, an average ranch house on a corner lot. It had no trees in front—nothing except grass, so nothing hid the splash stain that betrayed dirt and mold on the grey front brick—and three cars in the driveway. It was not run-down, but it didn't shine with any pride in ownership.

It also reeked of trouble. Rik parked two doors down and across the street, just a couple of doors from the proposed short-term rental at 12. Then she very carefully inched her phone up enough to photograph the corner house, number 20, and sent the picture to Kam.

But she didn't smell chemicals. She didn't feel them against her skin. Why did that house reek of despair and danger?

If someone hasn't died here, it's going to happen. It was like a powder keg.

Woman you get out of there that place has angry ghosts in it, said a text from Kam.

I think an abuser lives here and the ghosts hate him, Rik texted back. *We can't risk listing a property on this street. Poor neighbors.* Rik paused and then added: *Potential property 12 EDWest has bad mold. I have to tell them the house has too many allergy problems for BPI.*

Kam's response was thumbs-up and a stern face, to remind her to watch her back. Rik smiled and tucked her phone away, reaching for her respirator.

As predicted, the owner of number 12 was very unhappy to find out that the roofer hadn't bothered to mention the moldy beams in the attic that they probably found while reroofing. Rik explained that the mold was not the roofer's problem. She didn't add that they must not have had a kickback deal with any remodelers for referrals. She left the owner with an information sheet that would discourage them from trying again to get a Borrowed Places listing. Sad, sad situation.

As she locked her car doors, her cell phone rang. "Borrowed Spaces, Inc.," Rik said, hitting Speaker.

"Erika? This is Morgan."

"Hey, how are you? Come to any conclusions?" At this point Rik wasn't sure what to hope for, but she crossed her fingers, anyway.

"Ah, yeah, a place to start. After staying at the house until late...I think we should get rid of the immediate problem and do like October rentals? No more than four guest groups, and a day minimum between them?" Morgan started.

"Higher October rates, and a chance to see what your great-uncle's roommate thinks about things," Rik said without a pause, fumbling in the passenger seat for her clipboard and weekly planner. (A person affected by electromagnetic fields did not trust their calendar to anything electronic.)

"Yeah! Also, do you have time in the next few days to come see the bungalow? To see if we could do multiple rentals at once, or only entire house for festivals?" There was a thread of hope in Morgan's voice.

Hoping for more than one option, maybe? Smiling, Rik slid out her old pencil and clicked it open. "I'm sure we can find a time."

Once they'd agreed when to meet, Rik headed off to the next place on her list, a few exits south off the freeway. It was a neighborhood with many older live oaks, so she was looking forward to good landscaping.

As she slowed her car to approach the site, she heard barking and howling like an echo, even on a bright sunny morning. The spectral dog pack was hidden from her, but she heard, smelled, and *felt* ghosts. The chorus was enough confirmation.

As long as it didn't bother renters it was a bonus feature, because it added to "atmospheric" in the rating.

The house had a great steel roof, no mold, and beautiful native landscaping for the area. Inside, it was a mix of modern and old Formica fifties, decorated by an artist. And it had a laundry room! Priceless—it was surprisingly rare in this region to find a washer and dryer, but worth the added expense to renters who could not safely use a laundromat.

It also had several guardians protecting occupants.

Rik could see them in her mind's eye as she walked into the sitting room, as if someone had handed her a video shot at dawn. Four figures, barely more than shadows, from perhaps hundreds of years ago, tending a campfire and waiting for someone...

It was only a one-bedroom. Rik did not want to walk through that bedroom door... Her heartrate was fine, but there was definitely a cold spot at the hallway threshold. She could tell that the ghosts preferred that residents use the bath's hallway entrance by day and bedroom entry by night. Which was...curious.

Her phone clunked with a text, but she ignored it.

The homeowner who had met her was a tall, elegant man. His portrait hung high up on the living room wall of mixed paintings, suggesting his partner was the artist who decorated the house. "What do you think?" he said, his arms outstretched.

"I love it," Rik admitted. "It's a bit far out, the way the traffic patterns work, and that must be hurting you with other rental places, but I love it."

"It's hurting us," he admitted. "It's twenty minutes to downtown."

"Still, you're right by the river's boat launch, so your location is good for recreation," Rik continued, eyeing the threshold of the hallway door. "The futon in the living room means an extra queen bed. You've got Internet and a couple of streaming options—although your box buzzes, I would recommend changing that. Some guests are very sensitive to electromagnetic and mechanical sounds and frequencies."

"Now that's just conspiracy theory crap, isn't it?" he asked.

"If it's just conspiracy theory crap, how do I know that your cable box has an intermittency that buzzes, and that you have two fluorescent lamp ballasts on the property that are dying? One in the kitchen and the one in your laundry shed," Rik added, waiting to see how far she would have to push back. She didn't plan to tell this man that several shrouded spirits were quietly watching him, as if waiting for his answer.

The spirits had lingered here for hundreds of years. They didn't disapprove of the man, but they clearly weren't going anywhere. They had their mission, and it included protecting this site and those on it. *Okay.* Rik would not be so rude as to ask them why they lingered.

He hadn't mentioned the ghosts. People knew BPI rented both eco-clean and haunted places. If the owner hadn't felt or seen the ghosts, someone had.

Another text sounded. Honestly, she could go days without any messages, and then everyone wanted to text.

"Are the ballasts and the cable box the only problem?" he asked.

"So, you know BPI has two types of clientele, right? We have clients with allergies seeking safe rental locations for their health, and people curious about haunted houses. This place ticks off both boxes. Your ghosts seem protective. Have they ever been aggressive? If so, we recommend you have people sign a spectral waiver if you want both green and orange ratings," Rik told him. "Actually, for some people, signing that adds to the thrill."

The ghosts remained solemn. Rik sent them a mental message: *The leaders require agreement.* Their response was that one of them, a clan authority? Felt...approving, Rik thought.

The man shook his head, smiling. "Did someone tell you?"

"All I knew about this property is what is said about it on the other short-term rental sites," Rik decided to say.

"But Borrowed Places often gives a property a ghost rating," was his response.

"If a place rates one," Rik agreed.

"Well, there is *something* about this neighborhood," he said firmly. "We don't joke about it, but the last three owners of the house up the hill have all died while living there. And they weren't all elderly people, either. Also, my wife swears she hears a dog pack howling, but there's no dog pack out here in the hollows."

"But no one has died here recently." Rik waited.

"No, we haven't had anything weird like that here," he rushed on. "We do insist on insurance or a deposit."

"Not a problem," Rik assured him. "You also would need a spectral waiver in case the spirits in residence object to anyone using the hall bath entrance at night."

Now the man was staring at her. Then he glanced at the hallway and softly admitted, "Our dog barks at the bathroom door all the time."

Not the door, the threshold, Rik thought but didn't say aloud.

She was pretty sure she'd found another property.

The phone thunked a text again as she locked herself into her car. A quick look told her it wasn't a photo from her brother or from Kam—it was a whole string of texts from Mr. Emmons.

GHOST HAS GONE NUTS was the first message.

THROWING PECANS was the second message.

WONT LET US INTO HOUS had just come through.

Rik put her earbuds in, hit the Emmons number

and started her car. "Mr. Emmons, are you all right?"

"Saints preserve us; it's attacking me and Dolly!" The man sounded winded, and Rik could hear his wife's agitated shrieks in the background.

"What did you change?" Rik asked, pulling onto the highway.

"We didn't change nothin'!"

"You must have. The ghost's behavior has changed. First, we look at something you did—something you moved, or something you added—and then we consider if this manifestation is something that happens on a regular basis," Rik said, keeping her voice soothing.

"Can you come back now?" he yelled over his wife's comments. "Dolly says she's felt anxious the whole time she was here. All she was doing was cleaning with soap and water like you asked," he added.

"On my way," Rik assured him.

This time, she would let Kam know *before* she got out of the car. Just in case.

"Where did the pecans come from?" Rik asked, opening an umbrella and placing it on her shoulder. A fat pecan, still green in its spongy protective summer husk despite it being September, thumped against her thigh. Wincing, Rik faced the Emmonses. She'd found them huddled in their parking area, about twenty feet from their deck. Mr. Emmons's silver hair was disheveled, and Mrs. Emmons held up a folder to protect her face from the flying pecans. A bucket full of soapy water sat at her feet.

A pecan sailed by overhead. Rik was glad she had parked in the driveway by the road.

"There's a couple of pecan groves here. The Boone family grew pecans at one time," Mr. Emmons responded.

"What did you do?"

"Nothing!"

"Frank." Dolly Emmons was a small, wiry woman, sandalwood brown, with silver threading her dark hair. Her voice was very quiet, but when he heard his name, he calmed immediately.

Mrs. Emmons said, "Tell her what we did."

"We shouldn't." His voice was definite.

"It was legal," Mrs. Emmons replied. Her voice was steady. "We made the family sign off when they didn't want to take the ashes. You asked them, and they said it was fitting."

"What if that—that thing is gonna chase us and everyone off the property now?" Mr. Emmons wasn't yelling, but he was still upset, his mouth tight and a groove etched between his brows.

"Then we will go shovel up all that mulch between those two trees." Mrs. Emmons's tone was kind yet firm.

Rik was fairly certain she knew what had happened. "Where did you scatter the ashes?"

Mr. Emmons crossed his arms, his expression defiant. "We scattered them in the pecan grove next to the shed."

"And the cremains boxes? And the drawing? Where are they?"

He frowned, and gestured to the large trash and recycling bins neatly placed on a stone inset at the far end of the deck. "Boxes there. I kept the drawing for you like I said."

"So...did the pecan throwing start after you scattered the ashes? After you put the boxes in the trash? Can you pin it down?" Rik asked gently, trying not to flinch as another green-husked pecan flew by.

Mrs. Emmons looked thoughtful and Mr. Emmons remained angry. He waved his arms as several pecans thumped against his back. "They started flying when I put the boxes in the recycling bin. Those boxes are just cardboard!"

With a film of ashes on the surface, Rik thought but did not say.

"I was anxious in the house, earlier, but I usually feel that way in there," Dolly Emmons said slowly. "It's just sort of grown that way, over the weeks."

Thud! Rik winced, but the nut glanced off and didn't puncture her umbrella.

When the boxes were discarded... "Do you have the drawing, Mrs. Emmons?"

The woman handed Rik her file as she slid around behind her husband and covered her eyes.

Another pecan thumped against Rik's leg, but it felt half-hearted, as if lobbed in frustration. She opened the folder.

The drawing was in colorful markers, as if created by a kindergartner. The scene showed an older woman with glasses and white curls in some kind of chair, maybe a rocker, at the front entrance of a log house. No deck was shown, just grass...and a large star of yellow with orange edges next to her, easily as big as she was.

Like a sun or a galaxy.

Like...ghost energy?

"The people he loved best," Rik said thoughtfully. Was that whom the son had drawn, his mother and the ghost? She had heard of children seeing ghosts and making friends with them. Would a man with Down syndrome... Maybe he never stopped seeing his ghost friend.

"Is there a second person in the drawing?" Mrs. Emmons said aloud, peering under her cupped hands.

Maybe. Rik thought about it a moment. What if this was easy? The Emmonses had discarded the boxes, with only a trace of the last Boones left, but not the important part. Their spirits were not attached to those boxes.

Did the Boones linger? Was this chaotic energy one of the Boones...or the star?

What did a ghost sense? But did it need more than a dusty box to find them? *I'm sorry*, Rik thought. *I don't know if a part of their spirits stayed.* If any ghostly part of the woman and her son remained, might they be somehow anchored to their ashes?

Rik turned and faced the deck. "The Boones are in the grove," she yelled, pointing toward the shed. "The pecan grove! Check there."

A double handful of ripe pecans spilled at her feet.

Silence. No more pecans.

Rik waited.

As if carried by a breeze, she heard the sound of children laughing.

"Did it leave?" Mrs. Emmons had come up behind her and was peeking around her arm.

"Not necessarily. But it's not throwing pecans. That's a start." Rik extended the picture to the owner. "What if Mrs. Boone's son could see, or sense, the ghost? That's why he drew this energy?"

"Good heavens." Mrs. Emmons dropped her hands and took the picture. "I thought ghosts looked like people...if there really are ghosts."

"Do angels have wings?" Rik asked her.

The woman looked up, her mouth dropping open just a tiny bit. Then she closed her lips. "We know so little about creation," she whispered.

"We know that there is a lot we don't know," Rik suggested.

They all stood silent for a long moment.

"Would you like to see what we did after you left?" Mrs. Emmons finally said. "I wiped down everything with just water and that grease-cutting soap they use on oily seabirds."

"And I got my grandson to rip out all that bad wood in the basement," Mr. Emmons threw in. "He says we need to grade away from that side of the house properly for drainage, and put water seal on the foundation there before we repair the wood trim hiding the stone. He says someone makes a low VOC version that costs more but works fine?"

Rik smiled. So they were serious about this, for whatever reasons.

"You don't need this picture, do you?" Dolly Emmons asked her. "Maybe we could make a color copy of it and hang that here in the house."

"I'd like a photo of it. Maybe you could even give away postcards or sell prints," Rik said. "Put it next to a picture of you two, who have worked so hard to share this lovely place." Touching the drawing, she added, "I would keep this somewhere special, but maybe not in the house. You don't want anyone to decide it's a souvenir."

"Come look first at what we've done." Mr. Emmons waved them both toward the house.

"How about we do some pictures first?" Rik headed toward her car.

<hr/>

"My hair is a fright," Dolly insisted as her husband helped her up the steps to the deck and pulled her to his side.

"No, you look fine, happy, and like you've been working," Rik assured her, carefully focusing the square camera that held her high-speed film. It should take a picture of a couple before their short-term rental.

Or it might take even more. High-speed film was the gold standard for ghost hunters.

Rik could hear distant children laughing.

But the farm was isolated... "Who wants to be in the picture?" Rik called.

The couple gave her an odd look, but she held up a finger to them, feeling the cool tingle that sometimes told her something was different about the site. She caught a whiff of vanilla, like old, beloved cologne she knew from other houses. "We're going to take several at different angles," Rik said quickly, snapping one, and then moving the camera horizontally, leaving space to either side of Dolly and Frank Emmons. She tilted up and down, too, just to be sure.

And then Rik whipped out her cell phone for a couple of digital snaps.

"I'll show you the photos when they come back, and you can decide if you want to use them or not," Rik told them.

Dolly's expression was shrewd. "Can you see ghosts?"

"Almost never," Rik responded, putting away her phone.

"She thinks she feels them," Frank whispered to his wife.

Dolly looked up at him, astonished.

Rik snapped another high-speed picture.

"*Thinks?*"

The photos came back two days later, but Kam had already confirmed from the cell phone what Rik's eyes saw only on high-speed film or video. Smiling Dolly and Frank Emmons, looking both proud and a little embarrassed before their renovated farmhouse.

And to the couple's right, three orbs of energy, like camera flashes had gone off suddenly.

Rik smiled. She rather thought the Emmonses would get their Spectral Orange Star rating. *I wonder how the ghosts will let guests know that they are in residence.*

Here here here…

Still here.

At home.

Cat Kimbriel is working on a contemporary fantasy set in Austin, TX about curses, ghosts, and very different ways of looking at the twilight worlds. She's also working on a short Nuala piece and mulling over a new Alfreda novel. You can find her fantasy & science fiction, including free samples, at her Book View Café bookshelf. These books can also be found at major online booksellers. Her personal and very occasional blog is at Dreamwidth, and you will find her on whatever social media currently interests her. Cat builds worlds that contain compassion and justice— come join the journey.

About the story

Do you believe that a human being can run an English mile in about four minutes? If you believe the record is true—why do you believe it? How good are you at accepting that other people can do something you can't?

When someone hears something you don't—like a camera flash recharging? Do you doubt them? If not—

would you doubt them if they told you a kitchen light ballast was buzzing, driving them nuts?

If someone told you that an empty house felt "occupied"…do you immediately dismiss it? Wish you believed it? Wonder what it is they sense?

If. If. If.

I had the dubious privilege for decades of having a mostly unknown medical situation. To battle both medical gaslighting and becoming incapacitated, I had to go to incredible lengths to avoid certain foods, burning materials, mold in buildings, and VOC exposure. So I know something about not being believed.

Most people in my country scoff at ghosts. It's especially strange because most of the cultures of the world have a long history of belief in spirits, both dearly departed and "Others." Many countries still accept that large numbers of citizens believe in ghosts. Being a high tech country doesn't necessarily change this. After the Tohoku earthquake and tsunami of 2011 in Japan, hundreds of ghost sightings took place.

I listen when people tell me about a brush with a spirit. So I will say this about "Borrowed Places." Only one of the ghosts is made up. All the rest are disguised. People had ghost experiences, and you get the remix on them.

Enjoy that next vacation rental.

The Waking of Angantyr

Marie Brennan

Between one stroke of his hoe and the next, the farmer saw her.

The dying sun made her into a black silhouette, tall against the fiery sky. She paused for a moment at the top of the hill, then came his way with determined strides. He went on hoeing—little enough time left, before sunset—but kept a wary eye on her. Strangers had no reason to be here.

When she came within speaking distance, he stopped.

Her face was scratched and dirty, her blond hair hanging in tangled ropes. With a pack slung over one shoulder, she looked like a vagabond, but her bearing said otherwise. She radiated purpose. The farmer gripped his hoe more firmly.

Her eyes fixed on him, winter-blue against her grimy skin, and she spoke.

"Am I on Sámsey?"

"That you are," the farmer said, not relaxing. She didn't look like the survivor of a wreck. Kicked off some passing ship, maybe. "Where were you headed for?"

"Here," she said. For all her height, the farmer

realized, she was barely fully grown; beneath the dirt, her face was young. "I didn't know if I'd landed in the right place."

The farmer stared. "You were coming *here*? Sweet sun, what for? There's nothing on Sámsey but farms and ghosts!"

A twisted smile passed across her face—the smile of someone who has seen her fate and must either laugh or go mad. "So I've been told."

"You'll be needing shelter," the farmer said. Stranger she might be, but she seemed a harmless kind of crazy, and it was bad luck not to be kind to lunatics. "It's not far to sunset, and you don't want to be out at night. I don't know what possessed you to come to Sámsey, girl, but take my word—this isn't any kind of place for sane people. Most everybody has left. *I'd* leave, if I could."

She shook her head. "Thanks, but what I really need is directions. I'm looking for a burial mound."

"Sámsey's covered with them," he said. That was the whole problem.

"A specific one." She turned her head to gaze across the undulating ground of the island. "Thirteen men lie buried in it. A recent mound, built not more than fifteen years ago."

The farmer flinched. He didn't think she was looking at him, but she came alive at his reaction, moving suddenly closer. He retreated, holding his hoe like a defense. "Where is it?" she asked.

He shook his head, knowing already that he would lose this argument. Ragged as she was, she looked like one of *those* people—the sort who answered to a code that had nothing to do with common sense. But he had to try. "You don't want to go there, girl. This whole island's haunted, and that mound more than most. Come nightfall, it'll open up, and the flames will rise, and you don't want to be outside when that happens."

"Where is it?" she repeated, her voice iron-hard. As he had known she would.

Against his will, his arm rose to point. He knew the mound; everyone on Sámsey did. It lay on the island's southeastern edge, not far from where they stood.

She began walking that way immediately.

"How are you going to know which one it is?" the farmer called after her desperately.

"The ghosts will tell me!" she shouted back. "They brought me this far."

———————◆———————

Hervor found the mound shortly before sunset. It was easy to spot; thirteen men required a large barrow. She needed no ghostly voices to tell her that.

But they'd told her many other things. They had whispered to her in her sleep since childhood, murmurs of battle and betrayal and thirteen men murdered. That was how she knew their number. Finding out that they lay buried on Sámsey had not been so easy—ghosts, it seemed, were better at counting than geography—but she'd persevered. Because while she'd gotten used to dead men's voices in her sleep, lately they'd begun speaking to her in broad daylight. From that point on, it was clear: find them and silence them, or go mad.

She dumped the contents of her ragged pack onto the ground. Bones and leather and gleaming white stones tumbled out; she left them where they lay and pried an egg-sized rock out of the earth. Then she began to wander, ranging outward from the burial mound in growing arcs until she found a small hole, barely visible in the grass. From one pocket she produced an apple core, which she tossed down a few paces from the hole.

Then she crouched and waited.

Soon a twitching pink nose emerged from the burrow, followed a moment later by the rest of a skinny brown rabbit. The animal hesitated. Hervor didn't move. It hopped forward, paused, then darted for the apple core. The instant it stopped, Hervor threw her rock.

The furry body pitched over sideways. Hervor ran forward and grabbed it; the thing was only stunned, not dead, and it struggled as she bundled it into the tattered end of her shirt. The squirming was a nuisance, but she needed the rabbit alive.

Not for much longer, though. The sun was almost down.

Hervor returned to the burial mound, stuffed the rabbit into her now-empty pack, and began to lay everything out.

The rough square of leather she staked to the ground with four bones, one at each corner. Her hands shook; this was *draudr*, blood magic, and she'd heard enough tales of what could go wrong. There was a reason *draudr* was spoken of only in whispers—when it was spoken of at all. Getting the old woman to talk about it hadn't been easy.

But the crone's determination was nothing against Hervor's. This was the only way she would ever have peace.

So she steadied her hands and drew a circle on the leather, taking care to make the line solid and thick. In a few minutes, it would be the only thing keeping her safe. Best to be sure.

The circle drawn, she placed thirteen pale stones inside it, pale like the dead. One for each voice, each ghost, and a line to hold them in when the time came.

Madness, every bit of this. But she had only two choices: go on, or give up. And she could not give up.

Hervor laid her knife down on the leather. Then

she dragged the rabbit from the bag, where it was trying to chew its way free. She held the squirming animal in her arms and waited for the last sliver of sun to vanish below the horizon.

In the peculiar light of dusk, the barrow opened up.

There were no doors. The ground did not shift. Hervor was looking straight ahead at the grass, and then suddenly she saw through it to the chamber inside, where thirteen men sat cross-legged, their swords leaning against their shoulders, chill blue flames dancing around them and over their skin.

Their voices rose in her mind, whispers familiar from her earliest memories.

blood
betrayal
MURDER
lying cold
rivers of blood
and they're beyond our reach...

They sat in two ranks, six on a side, and the thirteenth faced her from the depths of the mound. The flames leapt higher around him, throwing his corpse-white face into hideous relief; his eyes glowed with the same blue light. He alone faced her, but he could neither see nor hear her. Not yet.

Hervor pinned the struggling hindquarters of the rabbit between her knees, stretched its neck over the leather square, and slit its throat.

The blood fountained over her knees and hands and the leather before her, drenching the white stones in red. For a moment it pooled in the center of the circle, unnaturally; then it drained into the thirteen stones, which began to glow with a sullen, bloody light. The four bones shone cold blue in response, the same blue as the barrow's flames.

The body of the rabbit fell to the ground, drained,

and then Hervor spoke the invocation the old woman
had taught her, using the names gleaned from so many
nights of dreams.

"Wake thou, Angantyr—Hervor wakes you.
Son of Arngrím, son of Grím,
son of Hergrím, hear me speak.
Rise from your grave; give me your words.

Sons of Angantyr, see me before you!
Hervard, Hjórvard, Hrani, Barri,
clad all in mail, I call you forth.
Death holds you not; I open the door.

Reifnir, Tindr, Tóki, Bófi,
white in your barrow, weapons in hand—
Búi, Haddingr, Brami, Saemingr!
Feast on the blood brought here for you.

Angantyr, warrior, wake to my call,
with blood and bone I bid you hear me.
Wake thou, Angantyr, answer my voice,
from the barrow-mound I beckon you forth!"

The thirteenth ghost stood.

Despite her determination, Hervor flinched back.
In his hand he held a sword, unsheathed: Tyrfing, the
blade famed in all the tales of Angantyr. The old
woman had said he could not harm her—none of them
could, not with the charcoal line holding them in—but
Hervor found it hard to trust. Was the sword ghostly,
or real?

But she had what she wanted; the ghosts, fed by
the rabbit's blood, could hear her. She must not waste
that. She must speak to them, if she wanted answers. If
she wanted peace.

"You've haunted my sleep for years."

Vengeance.

They spoke the word together. Hervor expected their lips would move, that she would hear them with her ears, but no—their disembodied voices echoed in her head as they always had, inescapable and cold. They'd never spoken of vengeance before, in all their years of whispering, but she wasn't surprised. What else would murdered men want?

"Why are you in my dreams?" she asked.

Sváfa's daughter.

That came from the thirteenth ghost alone. Angantyr. His frost-blue eyes held Hervor pinned. She trembled under his gaze, but made herself ask, "How do you know my mother's name?" Maybe ghosts just knew things.

Maybe not.

Angantyr came forward two steps, each one shivering the ground. *Why do you call us from the cold earth?*

"To silence you," Hervor said. The words limped from her, not nearly as strong as she'd meant them to be. "I'm sick of hearing you in my sleep, let alone when I'm awake. You want vengeance? Tell me who killed you."

Two eagles flew against us, the ghost of Angantyr murmured. *Battle in the sky. I will say no more.*

Hervor gritted her teeth. They could not haunt her for so many years, and then answer her only in riddles. "The honor of Arngrím's mighty line has turned to dust, if Angantyr and his sons fear to speak their killers' names."

The other ghosts murmured, their words indistinguishable. One by one their heads were turning to face her. At least they didn't stand. Hard enough to face Angantyr on his own.

Her insult, it seemed, struck home. *The eagles flew*

from the great lord's hall, Angantyr said at last. *His retainer Hjálmar, and Orvar the wanderer. The first stood against me, and the second, my sons.*

Two. Two men alone had been the end of Angantyr and his twelve berserker sons. And now they demanded vengeance.

Hervor was young and strong, but she'd been raised a bondsmaid. Hers had been a life of washing and cooking, not war. Orvar had killed Angantyr's twelve sons; Hjálmar had killed Angantyr himself, who—the stories said—was greater than his sons together.

Living with the voices didn't look so bad, when compared with certain death.

But how could she say that, after coming so far?

The blood of my line burdened the earth, Angantyr's spectral voice said. *One alone bears it now.*

A cold touched Hervor that had nothing to do with the barrow's chill. "What did you say?" she whispered, through nerveless lips.

The ghost's eyes seared like ice. *Daughter of Sváfa: you bear my blood.*

She was shaking her head before she even realized it. Angantyr's wife had been Tofa, not Sváfa, and Sváfa was her mother; even he admitted that. She couldn't be his daughter.

As if no one had ever been sired out of wedlock before.

Thus the voices, the dreams, the haunting since childhood. Who else would they cry to for vengeance, when all their other kin were dead?

Vengeance she couldn't give them. Hjálmar and Orvar would carve her to pieces; she didn't stand a chance.

But that wasn't the point. Honor was the point. If she was born of Angantyr's blood, she was no common thrall, and that meant she could allow herself no common weakness. In truth, she'd left that life behind a year ago, when she fled to seek out the ghosts and silence them. She'd already begun walking the path that blood laid out for her—which meant that honor must be her guiding force, now. Honor, and fate.

The gods had spun the skein of her life long ago. She would die either way, fighting or not. Or so they said. But the abstract idea of fate had never been so sharply real.

Hervor closed her eyes, searching for the courage to speak. Her head dipped, and when she opened her eyes, she found herself looking at her hands, streaked with rabbit's blood. Too much to hope it would some day be replaced by Hjálmar's. But she clenched her teeth and dragged her chin upward, intending to meet her father's eyes and speak the words honor demanded of her.

Her gaze stopped on his sword. Tyrfing, a blade as famous as the man who bore it.

A pointless gesture, perhaps—but if she was doomed, she might as well do it right.

"Give me your sword, and I will avenge you."

Silence. No answering whisper, no call for blood.

Hervor raised her eyes to meet her father's, and found his face as cold and forbidding as winter itself.

You court your doom, Angantyr said. *Your sense abandons you, when you come to the barrow and call up the dead. The spectral fires encircle you; death's domain beckons you in. Flee to your ship. Leave us in peace.*

"*What* peace?" Hervor cried, angered by his sudden dismissal. "Your murders have kept you lingering for fifteen years. And I have lingered *with* you, hearing your voices—but I will hear no more. Fires do not frighten me, though hellish their source; I have come through worse to find you tonight. I will take Tyrfing, to seek out your foes."

The blade gleamed in Angantyr's hand. *Listen, my daughter—hear my words out! Tyrfing, my sword, shall bring you no joy. Cursed it was, when first it killed. Let it stay in my barrow, lest ruin it bring to all of your kin.*

"I have no kin for it to ruin! My father lies murdered; my brothers lie with him. What have I to lose?" Hervor's hands clenched into fists, her nails cutting her skin.

Sons, Angantyr replied. *Disaster will this blade bring to you and your children, though you prevail against Hjálmar and Orvar.*

Hervor's breath died in her throat.

Hear thou, daughter, the character of this blade.

Behind Angantyr, his sons rose and drew their swords.

Deadly the edges; each carries poison. It shines as the sun, when it is unsheathed; fierce is this light, it betrays you to foes. Tyrfing may never be unsheathed without causing the death of a man, and it may not be sheathed again unless blood lies warm upon it.

Hervor stared at the blade. Yes, the stories had hinted of this—but they were just stories. People always exaggerated. But she did not think her father did. She did not think he *could.*

Nor was he finished. *This doom does it bear, from the hand of the gods: Tyrfing shall be the cause of three dishonorable deaths. But it will never turn on you, and so long as you bear it, blades will not cut you. Think this not a blessing: disaster it will bring to your sons, though honor you regain.*

His words threatened Hervor's fragile self-control, her newfound determination and courage. Against her will, a tear slipped free of her eye, tracking through the dirt on her face. Doom her sons, or fail her duty. What kind of choice was that?

Return to your home, Angantyr said. *Reach not for such pain.*

Pain. Either way she turned, she could not escape it. Would she even live to bear sons, if the ghosts kept haunting her, their murders unanswered? Or would she die, driven mad by this burden? What legacy would she give her sons, having failed in her duty as Angantyr's last kin?

Frustration and despair swamped her, dragging her spirit down. Hervor fled them, curling in on herself, reaching deep within for the strength that set her on this path in the first place.

She reached for strength, and found anger.

Anger at the two who had murdered the kinsmen she'd never known, damning her to a life as a bonds-maid. Anger at the gods who had cursed the blade, damning innocents to suffer for it. Anger at—at *everyone*, from her father to the farmer who thought she should hide inside and hope for safety. She faced her doom either way, but if so…

If so, she would face it on her feet, and regain her family's honor. Whatever the price.

Hervor stood.

She stepped over the bloodstained leather, came forward until she reached the very edge of the flames that encircled the mound. They sank low at her approach. Angantyr stood before her, separated only by the veil of blue light.

"Let my sons fend for themselves," Hervor said, no hint of tremor in her voice. "I have no dread of the doom you name. Not ghosts, nor gods, nor the flames of hell frighten me. Give me your sword. I will seek out the warriors that slew you and your sons. My father and brothers will rest in their graves before I am done."

Behind Angantyr, the twelve brothers she had never known stood arrayed, their swords in hand. In their dead eyes she saw pride, but in her father's she saw sorrow.

"Give Tyrfing to me," Hervor said. "I will find my own fate."

The cold blue fire grew in intensity until she had to close her eyes against its brilliance. When it faded, she found herself standing at the very base of the grassy mound. Dawn light came from the eastern horizon; night had passed without her knowing.

The sun glinted off something at the top of the mound.

Tyrfing.

Hervor stood, trembling. The blade lay in the grass, there for the taking. A chance to find peace.

If she was lucky. If she was strong enough.

Hervor climbed to the top of the mound and picked up the sword. As she touched it, the blade began to shine with its own light, rivaling that of the sun.

Her sons would be born of an honorable line. Whatever their fate, they would face it on their own.

Marie Brennan is a former anthropologist and folklorist who shamelessly pillages her academic fields for inspiration. She recently misapplied her professors' hard work to *The Night Parade of 100 Demons* and the short novel *Driftwood*, and together with Alyc Helms as M.A. Carrick, she is the author of the Rook and Rose epic fantasy trilogy, beginning with *The Mask of Mirrors*. The first book of her Hugo Award-nominated Victorian adventure series The Memoirs of Lady Trent, *A Natural History of Dragons*, was a finalist for the World Fantasy Award. Her other works include the Doppelganger duology, the urban fantasy Wilders series, the Onyx Court historical fantasies, the Varekai novellas, and over sixty short stories, as well as the New Worlds series of worldbuilding guides. For more information, visit swantower.com, her Twitter @swan_tower, or her Patreon at https://www.patreon.com/swan_tower.

About the story

I came across the Old Norse poem "The Waking of Angantyr" while doing research for my senior thesis in college, and it immediately seized my imagination. Ghosts? Swords? A warrior maiden? Tell me more! It turns out there *is* more, in the form of the saga the poem is found in; that's known by a variety of titles, one of which is *Hervarar saga*, making it one of the only Norse epics named after a woman.

Unfortunately, when I went and read the saga itself, I found myself resoundingly disappointed. Contrary to the editorial notes in the book where I first read the poem, Hervor does *not* go off with the sword Tyrfing and get revenge for her father. Instead, she basically goes home and that's the end of her story; the saga continues on with her son, Heiðrek. This irritated me so much that I went and wrote a (currently trunked) novel to do better by her…but first I wrote a short story.

One which takes some liberties with the source material, to be sure. Apart from the implication that Hervor intends to do a lot more than just go home and have a kid, I changed things so that the other murdered men are *her* brothers, not Angantyr's. But the fingerprints of the original are still very much there—not least in the fact that keen eyes may spot a distinctive alliterative pattern in much of Angantyr's dialogue, reflecting the style of Old Norse poetry.

It All Ends with a Game of Croquet

Jill Zeller

The day my husband walked into the pantry and didn't come out again was not that unusual. It happens all the time. Our pantry is under the stairs. *Ah, yes, of course,* you nod. Everyone knows that under-the-stairs spaces are by their nature portals to the Other.

He'll be back, I remember thinking, with the rolled oats in time for the granola baking.

Our tenants don't like it when we bake granola. The combined aroma of coconut flakes, toasted millet and of course the rolled oats seems to upset them. I hear them complaining but it's never to me. I don't have time for people who are confrontation-averse. Let them suffer, if they're not going to come to me about it.

My husband feels differently but that's his sweet nature. He doesn't like to needle the tenants as I do, and he doesn't like it when I do. Also it's my fault that we are in this situation in the first place, with strangers sharing our house. But my husband doesn't blame me. He tries to comfort me when I spiral into the dark, oily place of self-pity, like I'm rappelling into the deepest cavern on earth. His reluctance to intervene is not because he loves me, it's because things get really bad for our tenants when I'm in the throes of tortuous self-recrimination.

As usual, while I wait for him to come back from his portal jaunt, I go out into the garden.

The summer days have been blistering hot, and the tenants are not outside. I saw the wife out early this morning, watering her tomato plants and roses. At least the tenants like to garden and the backyard has never looked better. It's a very large yard, bordered by a copse where I sit when I'm agitated. The voices of the trees soothe me. This development of the oaks speaking to me and each other is new, just like the east wind that stirs the hot air today. I am lucky that the tenants never come out this far—at least when I am here. It's fine with me.

Only twice before has my husband gone through the portal without telling me. I try not to mind. An absent-minded sort, he probably remembered something he wanted to do and just did it. The shade cools me; the trees are sleepy right now and not in the mood for conversation. I shouldn't be baking granola in the middle of the afternoon, but I'm bored. We already have several bags of it stashed in the freezer.

My husband thinks some of the bags have gone missing. I wonder about him sometimes—is he getting senile? Who's counting, anyway? Probably the tenants took some. Again, I try not to care, but I wish they would ask.

I hear a car pull into the driveway alongside the house. It's probably the tenants' son; he's twenty or so, on summer vacation from college. I don't like him. He's nosy, and acts as if he wants to get to know us. My husband knows I don't like strangers but he's always friendly to the kid. I've watched him from the upstairs window, playing croquet with the kid in the garden.

The son also likes to come into my copse. Getting up, I walk back to the house, looking at the sky or the ground, pretending not to care whether someone is watching me. I straighten a leaning gnome. I shift some gravel from the walk with my foot.

Probably my husband is back. I go into the kitchen, but it is still empty. No husband. No rolled oats.

I hear loud voices, giggling; the son has brought his girlfriend over. *Worser and worser.* I feel irritation building. It hardens my lips, flares my nostrils. I know that ordinarily I would just sigh and turn on the stereo, but because my husband still isn't back I'm jumpier than ever.

Choosing a CD, I slip it into the player and turn up the volume.

Oddly, I can hear the son and his mother talking, as if they are standing next to me. This has happened before, and I figure it's furnace ducts or an echo.

"Where's that music coming from?" the son asks.

The wife's voice is soft, almost a whisper. "It's them."

"Oh, wow." This must be the girlfriend. But she's a new one. Her voice at least isn't as nasal as the one before her.

"It's really loud. Do they do this often?"

The wife sighs. "Oh, it's not too bad. I like the music."

This irritates me even more. I stop the CD, pull another from the shelf.

"Oh, it stopped," says the girl.

"Just wait," says the wife.

I laugh out loud. *Yeah, just wait.*

I hit play. I hear them groan as one.

The wife says, "Oh, no, not that old guy. Ick, it's nauseating."

Just as I was intending.

"Wow," says the girl.

After they leave the house, going out to dinner together, I turn off the music and sit at the kitchen table. I used to smoke and I think this would be a great time to light up, but I don't have any cigarettes. I'll bet that boy has some. He carries the faint odor of nicotine.

I go into their apartment and nose around. They are kind of sloppy, dust on the side tables and the kitchen nook is littered with a cereal box, and bowls, an empty milk carton. I should just clean this up, I think, but I don't touch anything. They would be so upset.

But I do find a vape pen in the bathroom. It's pink. Must be the girlfriend's. My opinion of her drops down a few notches. It's loaded, and I go back to my kitchen, and take several puffs.

Immediately I feel calmer, but still vaguely alarmed. *Where is he?* I occupy myself by taking the pen back to their bathroom, rearranging a few of the framed photos in their hallway on my way, and return to the empty kitchen.

It's been several hours. He's never been gone this long before. The sun is deep in the west, as if blown there by the wind. The crickets are beginning to sing.

I go to the pantry door, still ajar. Swallowing, I wipe my hands, which have begun sweating. I feel my heart begin to race. Probably the smokes, I tell myself, but I know it's not that.

It's that I have never entered the pantry before, not once since I learned about the portal.

The pantry is small, and to get to the portal one has to bend real low, this little room being under the stairs. I bump my head as I step toward the low wall at the pantry's end.

I crouch, my knees groaning. It's very warm here, like a sauna. How do our stored sacks, cartons, boxes, jars and cans ever keep as long as they do? *Where is he?*

Why does he do this to me?

Whatever is beyond the wall, a plain, white wallboard wall, frightens me more than anything I can remember. I badly desire, and at the same time abhor, the thought of going through, as if all the horrific memories of a lifetime will be piled out there for me to see and not ever unsee.

Time doesn't behave as expected in the pantry, and when I have had enough of squatting and shaking, back away from the wall, and step into the cool kitchen, it is dark.

I hear voices. The tenants are back.

The thought of talking to the tenants, to ask if they have seen my husband, makes me sick and cold. Also, if he has left me at last, I don't want them to know. I couldn't stand the shame.

I move into the living room, the best place to eavesdrop on the tenants. They are laughing, joking back and forth. I hear the refrigerator door open and close, the tinkling of ice into glasses. The son and the girl go out onto the back deck. I hover just out of view at the window to watch. The girl is vaping, using her pink pen. A cloud of exhaled mist flows from her mouth, looking like so much ectoplasm.

Maybe they aren't really there. Maybe they are just ghosts after all and I can have my house back to myself.

The boy's parents appear, the husband carrying a tray with a cocktail pitcher and glasses. They bring the party home, I think as I watch the wife pour yellow liquid for all.

The next moment my heart freezes. I become a stone with a gaping mouth as I see my husband coming across the lawn from the copse.

The tenants wave him over, laughing with greetings. The wife offers him a cocktail and he takes it, then settles himself on a lounge chair.

Without knowing, I have moved closer to the window. It clouds up with my breath.

"The garden looks great," my husband says, after a sip.

The tenant-husband flourishes his hand toward his wife. "She is the goddess of the garden. It's all her."

The wife looks down, shakes her head, but I can see her smile with pride. My back feels rigid with anger. "It's all luck, really."

"Oh, Mom." The son has his arm around the girl, who is perched on the arm of his chair. "C'mon. This place was a weedy mess when you moved in. Sorry, sir," he says to my husband, who is nodding in friendly agreement. "But there wasn't much going on out here back then."

"We are not green-thumb people. My wife doesn't even allow house plants because they all die."

My wife has a black thumb, is what he has not said.

I feel betrayed. And I feel guilty about it. He knows how shy I am, how I hate most people, and yet I can't deny him the chance for company when he can get it. What I don't like is how he engineered this little visit—the portal must have something to do with it. And he didn't even tell me this was what he wanted to do.

"I'd like to meet her, to thank her for making this such a wonderful place to live," says the tenant-wife. I feel my jaw ache as I grind my teeth.

A brief silence falls on the group. From the woods crickets sing. Their faces are lit by the lights the tenants have strung along the deck and patio, making a sparkling micro-universe right here beside my house.

"Mom." The son leans forward. "Look behind you. There she is."

I duck away from the glass, but not before they all see me.

When my husband returns I am waiting in the dark kitchen, sitting at the table, folding and unfolding my napkin. I can see him grinning in the dark.

"Oh, that was fun," he says as he sits opposite me.

I make no reply. Fold. Unfold.

Taking a deep sigh, he leans back, puts his hands behind his head. "They are such nice people. The son is studying theater. And the wife acted on Broadway, did you know that?"

Unfold. Fold.

"I don't know how they keep their spirits up so well. After all that happened to them. His fight with cancer, the wildfire that destroyed their retirement home. Yet, they always seem to look at the bright side."

Fold. "They laugh too much. I think people who laugh too much are just nervous."

My husband straightens in his chair. "Really, you should come with me next time. It would do you good to be around people."

"I hate people."

"I know. I know." He reaches toward my hand but I move it away. "You don't have to be around hateful people ever again. Just give these people a chance."

We don't speak about it for several days. The newest batch of granola is in the freezer and I start keeping track of them. I do find that some are missing.

After the son and his girlfriend leave, the tenants are very quiet. I am on edge for days, worrying the wife will attempt to visit me. But she hasn't tried yet.

My husband doesn't use the portal for the next three weeks. I watch the wife working in the garden, trying to see what her secret is. How does she keep all these plants alive? How does she get them to be so huge and verdant and prolific with blooms? They perfume the air; I can even smell them inside. I have never seen so many birds before.

I drift into the dining room, where my husband has commandeered the dining table for his diorama. He fills his days with constructing tiny houses, boats, vehicles, and minute people for his reconstruction of our little magic town. Recently he has hung lights from the ceiling, along with a couple glowing planets, and is fussing about how to make a comet skim through the lights—stars—every hour.

Our house is there in the micro-town, at the end of the dead-end street, at the border of the forest. He is working carefully on the garden, reconstructing the wife-tenant's landscaping.

He makes his models from paper and resin and daubs of paint, all applied at the desk in the living room, where he has a magnifying glass and bright lights and tweezers and clamps the size of insects.

"I'm going through the portal again. I want to take a closer look at the garden," he says, squinting at a spiky green blob that will evolve into a flowery shrub.

I stand in the archway, sighing.

"Come with me."

"Why should I?" I try to make my voice hard, but it sounds whiny.

He puts down the blob and peers at me over his magnifying glasses.

"Because they want to meet you. They're not afraid of you."

"What if I'm afraid of them?"

He cocks his head. "You have to know we have the advantage here. When they understood the situation, our terms, they accepted it. They're very open people.

They're curious about us."

I sigh again. I hate them being here. It's been three years now. I know I have to also be accepting, but I don't think I have it in me.

He smiles kindly. I hate that.

"When they saw some of the things you do," he says, rolling his blob under his finger, "they were afraid at first, but I explained how things are, and now they seem delighted. When you leave a book in their bathroom, when you switch the chairs around in their living room, when you wash their dishes, they laugh and think how sweet it is."

"It's anything but *sweet*," I snarl.

He laughs to himself now. I feel like I am the outcast, the mean one, the hater. How did I get this way? I watch my husband shrug and go back to his blob.

I am expecting it, and yes, late in the afternoon he goes through the portal.

I watch through the window.

The tenants are gathered in the garden. They've set up the croquet game. My husband ambles toward them from the copse, hands in his pockets. They greet him with hugs. I am so angry I could cry. My eyelids burn.

The son's car purrs into the driveway. There comes the multiple slamming of car doors, as if he has brought a bunch of kids with him. But I only hear the giggling laughter of the girl along with the son's baritone. Their feet crunch on the gravel.

"They're here!" The wife claps her hands.

The three of them turn to watch the side yard as the son and his girl come through the gate. The girl is carrying something. Her back is partly turned to me and as I watch, the faces of my husband and the tenants light up in big smiles.

"Oh, how adorable," the wife cries, and walks to the girl and takes the bundle from her.

I freeze. *No. They can't do this to me. It's not fair.*

I feel my husband's gaze on me, but I am staring at what the wife is holding.

Leaning my face against the glass, I feel the tears start. My heart is a throbbing, painful balloon.

This is the one thing my husband knows I resent more than anything. When everything changed, and we realized what had happened, this one grief and regret loomed large for me.

The wife places the bundle on the grass, and through my blurry tears I see the puppy as a wiggling blob, running back and forth among them, licking faces, giving out small yaps of joy. It is a chocolate Lab, maybe twelve weeks old, stumbling and weaving on chubby legs.

Only my husband knows how much I've missed having the dogs around.

I sit on the floor, my chin on the sill, watching them and the puppy as the night folds over, the micro-universe glimmers above them, the breeze softens, the tree frogs begin to sing.

After several hours, and a quick buffet dinner outside on the deck, the son and his girl get up to leave. I wish they would stay, so I can watch their dog scamper around the garden picking up twigs and shaking them.

But the unthinkable happens. They leave, but they don't take the puppy with them. The husband-tenant holds the dog in his arms as he bids goodbye.

My husband nods. They are speaking softly.

"I think this might do it," my husband says.

"I sure hope so," the wife says.

When my husband returns, I am still at the window. My knees ache but I don't have the power to move. He kneels and gives me a close hug. I sob into his shoulder.

Over the next several days I hear the dog about the house, her barks, her nails on the flooring, the back door opening to let her out and closing behind her as she runs back inside. My husband says nothing about the dog to me; he works on his diorama, reads, does the crossword. I haven't made granola since the dog came. I haven't gone into the tenants' apartment to alphabetize their vinyl records.

One morning dawns with valley fog. The yard is misted with it. I know before my husband does that he is going through the portal today. And right after breakfast, he enters the pantry without a word. I wait, knowing he will not return with a jar of pickles.

After a century of waiting which is only five minutes, I get up, grab my sweater, and open the pantry door.

The white wall portal entry waits for me in the darkness. I don't turn on the pantry light. I bump my head on the lowering ceiling as I walk toward it.

I don't even know how to use the portal. I never asked my husband to show me and he's never offered. But it has to be easy. It doesn't require "open sesame" or brute force, I surmise. On my knees, I lay my hand on it and my hand goes through, as though I am pushing aside a heavy velvet drape.

Crawling, my head and shoulders move easily. My heart is thumping; I am holding my breath. It is very cold, but only for a few seconds.

When I emerge from the velvet, mist breathes on my face. I feel it! Soft tiny fingers of moisture. To have skin again is remarkable. No wonder my husband is happy when he returns from his jaunts.

Standing up, feeling the cold—yes, I grabbed my sweater but old habits, even when you are dead, are hard to drop—I find myself in the copse. My husband waits there, his face split wide by a grin. He comes and envelops me in his arms.

I ask his shoulder, "Do all ghosts have portals like this?"

"I've no idea." My husband's chest rumbles as he speaks. "It called to me, though. I had just realized what happened to us. It took you longer, because of the trauma of the accident, I suppose, and for which you stupidly blame yourself. It called to me and I found myself on my hands and knees pushing on wallboard that gave way like warm, thick water."

"I'm scared."

"Me too."

He gently steers me from the copse, and we cross the foggy garden. The croquet game is still set up.

I love croquet.

The puppy sees us from the window, sets up a happy bark. This brings the tenants out the back door, and they wait on the deck as we come near.

"I've been waiting for this," the wife says, offering me her hand. I take it. It's warm and slightly sticky. "We were thinking of bringing in a medium, to help us contact you—I'm glad we didn't have to do that. It's so traumatic for ghosts."

"How did you know we were here?" My voice sounds small, girlish.

The wife smiles. "I saw your husband one night, as I walked into the copse looking for mushrooms. I recognized him right away from the newspaper photographs. I felt so bad for both of you, getting all the way to the top of Mount Rainier, then dying from a fall into a crevasse."

"We knew this had been your house. Your daughter told us when she saw us here with the realtor." This from the husband.

The puppy thunders toward me. She has grown inches in these short weeks, it seems to me. As heavy as she is now, I pick her up and she slathers my face.

"My daughter has our dogs now," I say, feeling the first laugh coming. I am the ghost who laughs, I think.

The tenant husband says, "I hope you don't stop changing little things. My wife really needs someone to organize the papers she piles all over her desk."

We all laugh at this.

"My son loves the granola," the wife adds.

I look up to where blue sky hangs above the shredding fog. My husband will tell me the rules of the portal, when and how long we can be visible, in our flesh. I do like the ability to walk through walls and hear every last word uttered by the house and the trees. But in the meantime—

"Shall we play some croquet before breakfast?" My husband picks up a mallet.

He hands it to me. In one hand I feel soft warm fur, in the other cool strong wood.

"Watch out," my husband says as we march toward the croquet field, the puppy bouncing beside us. "She's wicked at croquet. We're all about to lose."

Author of numerous novels and short stories, **Jill Zeller** is a Left Coast writer, second generation Californian, retired registered nurse, and obsessed gardener. Her works explore the boundaries of reality. Some may call it fantasy, but there are rarely swords and never elves. More to the point, she prefers to write as if myth, imagination and hallucination are as real as the chair she is sitting on as she writes this.

She lives in Oregon with her patient husband, two silly English mastiffs, and two rescue cats—the silliest of them all. Find more about Jill and her books at www.jillzeller.com.

About the story

We have a pantry very like the one in the story. It isn't a portal, as far as I know, except a portal to inspiration. A house is one of my most favorite characters. Houses "people" my stories and novels, making decisions, performing magic, manipulating lives. "It All Ends with a Game of Croquet" came to me as I thought about that pantry in my own house.

My process, when starting with a new idea, begins with "writing into the dark". A new idea may, like all my historicals, be rooted firmly in a historical event, or a new idea may be nothing at all. Like coming up with a ghost story for this anthology. For this, I started with a pantry, a pantry with a portal. Once I had my character, a nameless woman, middle-aged, bearing grudges and issues with the tenants, the story began to evolve. Many times, all I have to do is introduce a dog, and the story takes off.

Every story is about desire, need, choice, memory. Characters carry these weights and shed them, or not. These are essential, but for me, an element of the other-worldly makes the tale far more interesting. In this story, I tested myself to see if I could spin things a bit with point of view and perception. Hopefully, if I have succeeded, the reader will enjoy the trip.

About the Editors

Marissa Doyle has never actually *seen* a ghost, but has definitely heard them (though the one in her house is quiet and kindly.) But she loves ghost stories of all descriptions, so she's very pleased that her first foray into anthology editing was a ghost story collection. On the writing side, she's hopelessly addicted to writing historical fantasy for adults and young adults, including the *Leland Sisters* series beginning with *Bewitching Season,* and the just released *What Lies Beneath.* She is an ever-hopeful gardener, a slightly slapdash quilter, and an avid antique hunter, and lives in her native Massachusetts with her family.

Visit her at www.marissadoyle.com to learn more about her books.

Shannon Page was born on Halloween night and spent her early years on a back-to-the-land commune in northern California. A childhood without television gave her a great love of the written word. Edited books include anthologies *Witches, Stitches & Bitches*, the *Book View Café 2020 Holiday Anthology*, *Black-Eyed Peas on New Year's Day*, *Murmurs in the Dark* (with Marissa Doyle), and the essay collection *The Usual Path to Publication*, as well as novels for Per Aspera Press, Ragnarok, and Outland Entertainment. She has also authored a number of books under several different names—including her own—along with dozens of short stories.

Shannon is a longtime yoga practitioner, has no tattoos (but she did recently get a television), and lives on lovely, remote Orcas Island, Washington, with her husband, author and illustrator Mark J. Ferrari. Visit her at www.shannonpage.net.

Other Book View Café Anthologies

It Happened at the Ball, edited by Sherwood Smith

Book View Café 2020 Holiday Collection, edited by Shannon Page

Black-eyed Peas on New Year's Day, edited by Shannon Page

Spawn of Rocket Boy and Geek Girl, edited by Phyllis Radford and Shannon Page (coming soon)

About Book View Café

Book View Café is an author-owned cooperative of professional writers, publishing in a variety of genres including fantasy, science fiction, romance, mystery, and more.

Its authors include New York Times and USA Today bestsellers as well as winners and nominees of many prestigious awards such as the Agatha Award, Hugo Award, Lambda Literary Award, Locus Award, Nebula Award, RITA Award, Philip K. Dick Award, World Fantasy Award, and many others.

Since its debut in 2008, Book View Café has gained a reputation for producing high quality books in both print and electronic form. BVC's e-books are DRM-free and distributed around the world.

Book View Café's monthly newsletter includes highlights on new releases, specials, author news, and event announcements. To sign up, please visit https://bookviewcafe.com/bookstore/newsletter/